ALSO BY KATE BANKS

Howie Bowles, Secret Agent

Howie Bowles and Uncle Sam

PICTURE BOOKS

Spider Spider

Baboon

And If the Moon Could Talk

A Gift from the Sea

The Bird, the Monkey, and the Snake in the Jungle

The Night Worker

The Turtle and the Hippopotamus

Close Your Eyes

Dillon

Dillon

Dillon
Dillon

KATE BANKS

Frances Foster Books
Farrar, Straus and Giroux
New York

I would like to acknowledge my indebtedness to the painstaking and thorough research of Judith W. McIntyre in her study of loons and their behavior (*The Common Loon: Spirit of Northern Lakes* [Minneapolis: University of Minnesota Press, 1988]). And I would like to pay homage to the traditions of oral storytelling which, through legend and lore, have nurtured and perpetuated the magic of these intriguing birds.

Copyright © 2002 by Kate Banks
All rights reserved
Distributed in Canada by Douglas and McIntyre Ltd.
Printed in the United States of America
Designed by Nancy Goldenberg
First edition, 2002
10 9 8 7 6 5 4

Library of Congress Cataloging-in-Publication Data
Banks, Kate, 1960–
    Dillon Dillon / Kate Banks.— 1st ed.
        p. cm.
    Summary: During the summer that he turns ten years old, Dillon
Dillon learns the surprising story behind his name and develops a
relationship with three loons, living on the lake near his family's New
Hampshire cabin, that help him make sense of his life.
    ISBN 0-374-31786-0
    [1. Identity—Fiction.   2. Family—Fiction.   3. Adoption—Fiction.
4. Vacations—Fiction.   5. Loons—Fiction.   6. Birds—Fiction.
7. Lakes—Fiction.   8. New Hampshire—Fiction.]   I. Title.

PZ7.B22594 Di 2002
[Fic]—dc21

                                                            2001033207

For my parents

Dillon
Dillon

1

EACH OF US has a story and it starts with a name.

What kind of parents would name their child Dillon Dillon? Parents who were witless or unkind? Parents who could not feel? Parents who had forgotten that a name was the first thing you wore against your raw naked skin? Dillon's parents were not like that. Dillon's parents were smart. They were nice. They would not do a thing like that. Not on purpose.

Everyone makes mistakes. Dillon knew it was a mistake to put pencil shavings in Louis Gottlieb's milk carton at snack time. Ms. Ryan's fourth-grade class was learning square roots. And in a moment of rare genius Louis realized that Dillon Dillon could be neatly reduced to a square root symbol. Louis knew it was a mistake to share this revelation with his classmates. But he did it anyway. He pointed to Dillon and he cried out, "D squared."

"Raise your hand if you have something to say," said Ms. Ryan.

Louis raised his hand and smiled gleefully. "Dillon Dillon. D2," he said this time. The entire class laughed loudly, all except Dillon, who sank lower in his chair and began sharpening a pencil. His concentration drowned out the chorus of "D2" that followed as two-thirds of his pencil was eaten away. Dillon emptied the shavings into a paper cup. At snack time he dumped them into Louis Gottlieb's milk carton. Louis nearly choked to death when he drank his milk. Ms. Ryan had to perform the Heimlich maneuver. And she kept Dillon after school. She had not felt the ripple in her heart that Dillon felt when the other children began shouting "D2." Maybe that was because she read automobile magazines and she knew that all the hot new cars had names like Z8 or A6. Still, a boy is not a sedan or a convertible.

As far as Dillon was concerned, his name was practically responsible for Louis Gottlieb's nearly choking to death. This was a mistake. Dillon had said he was sorry. He hoped Louis would forgive him. But Louis had called him a "carcass." Dillon didn't know what that meant. When he got home he looked it up in the dictionary. According to the dictionary, carcass was "a dead body; the decaying or worthless remains of a structure . . ." There was more, but Dillon didn't bother to read the rest.

Dillon's parents did not tell him about his name until he turned ten. Maybe this was a mistake. They had planned to tell him sooner. They had been waiting for the right moment. But as so often happens in life, the right moment never came.

2

DILLON WAS A "HOPER." That was one of the nice things about him. There were many nice things about Dillon, but he wasn't aware of them. He could never get past that name, never get to know himself. Still, he kept on hoping. Hoping that one day this might change. Hoping that he'd be forgiven for nearly killing Louis Gottlieb. Hoping that if he filled in the coupons on the backs of all the cereal boxes he'd eventually win something. Dillon's older brother, Didier, thought this was stupid. Didier was thirteen. He was a realist.

"Stop wasting ink, Dill," he said. "Nobody

ever wins. It's a trap to get you to buy revolting cereal that will rot your teeth."

Dillon listened patiently to his brother, but he kept on writing. "Someone has to win," he said. "It says so right here." Dillon lifted up the cereal box and read out loud, "More than one hundred prizes drawn!"

"And what makes you think that of all the suckers buying cereal and filling in those coupons you would win?" asked Didier.

"Why not?" said Dillon.

"What's a sucker?" asked Daisy. Daisy was Dillon's little sister. She had just turned five.

"A lollipop," said Mrs. Dillon. She frowned at Didier. "Isn't that right?" she said.

Dillon looked at his mother admiringly. Then he turned to Didier.

"It says here that the first-prize winner gets a free trip to Disneyland," continued Dillon. "For the entire family."

"I wouldn't get my hopes up, honey," said Dillon's mother.

Didier snorted. "Do you know how many coupons they receive?" he asked.

"No," said Dillon.

"Millions," said his mother.

"Billions," said Didier.

"Trillions," added Daisy.

Dillon kept on writing. He kept on hoping. When he was finished, he cut the coupon carefully along the dotted line and sealed it in an envelope. He put a stamp in the corner and walked to the mailbox at the end of the driveway.

Dillon liked going to the mailbox. He liked pulling down the door flap and reaching for the letters. He liked sorting through them to see if there was something for him. Except for the coupons he sent in, he rarely wrote to anyone. And no one wrote to him. Still, Dillon kept on hoping that one day he would find something addressed to him:

Dillon Dillon
1687 Geller Road
Rock Falls, New Hampshire 03877

Dillon lifted out the bundle of letters. He shuffled through them quickly. There was nothing for him. Then he walked to the end of his street and dropped his own letter into the corner mailbox, in the slot for out-of-town letters.

Days passed. Weeks. At school Dillon moved happily from square roots to long division. He did not forget about the coupon. But it was no longer in the forefront of his thoughts. Instead it dangled somewhere in the back of his mind on a small fading thread of hope. Far enough away so that when at last the response came, Dillon was taken by surprise.

3

Mr. Dillon Dillon
1687 Keller Road
Rock Falls, New Hampshire 03877

THAT'S WHAT THE ENVELOPE SAID. They'd gotten the name of his street wrong. Dillon had
never heard of Keller Road. And he hardly
thought of himself as a mister. But he was sure
the letter was meant for him. There was cer-
tainly no other Dillon Dillon in Rock Falls, or
anywhere else in the world for that matter.

Dillon tore open the envelope. It was from
the cereal company. Out of all the millions and
billions and trillions of coupons sent in, his had

been drawn. He had won something. Not a little something like a Super Ball or a key chain. He had won first prize. He had won an all-expenses-paid week at Disneyland for his entire family.

Dillon read the letter again and again. He could not believe it.

"I won!" he cried.

"What did you win?" asked Didier. "A Mickey Mouse pencil?"

Dillon ignored his brother. "I won a trip to Disneyland," he said. "Remember the coupon I sent in?"

"Let me see," said Didier. Dillon handed Didier the letter. Didier read it out loud. He read it again. After the third time he put the letter down. "Way to go, Dillon," he said.

"We can go, can't we, Mom?" asked Dillon.

Dillon's mother picked up the envelope. She didn't look hopeful. "There are no dates," she said. "And you still have to fill this out." She handed Dillon a questionnaire with two full sheets of queries. It had to be completed and returned within two weeks. When the cereal company received it, they would send out further information.

Dillon sat down and began answering each question: Had he ever been to Disneyland? Why did he want to go? Was this the first time he'd won anything? What were the names and ages of his family members? And so on. When Dillon had completed the form, he folded it and stuffed it into the enclosed return envelope. Just as he'd done six weeks earlier, he walked to the end of his street and dropped it in the corner mailbox.

Dillon waited one month. Two months. The further information never came. At the cereal company a new employee had mislaid Dillon's envelope. She was asked to send a letter and another questionnaire to Dillon, but she forgot. Dillon tried the 800 phone number on the back of the cereal box countless times, but he was always placed on hold.

"It was probably just a publicity hoax," said Didier.

"Or a mistake," said his mother. "Everyone makes mistakes. Isn't that right?" she added cheerfully. Dillon nodded.

In any case, the free trip to Disneyland fell to the second-place winners, Mr. and Mrs.

Clarence Witherspoon and their two daughters, Lottie and Claire.

"It's not the end of the world," said Dillon's father. "We'll go up to the lake like we always do."

Dillon was not listening. He had not clutched the prize in his hand for long enough to feel truly disappointed. On the contrary, he felt strangely elated. He had won something. A big something. And nothing could take that away.

When the time came to leave for Lake Waban, Dillon packed his suitcase. He sat on top of his luggage and snapped the latch shut. As the car pulled out of the driveway, Dillon knew he was headed for the lake. But being the hoper he was, he continued to hope that by some strange twist of fate he might end up at Disneyland.

4

THE ROAD CURVED like a lazy river, pitching Didier into Dillon and squashing Daisy against the door of the car. Dillon had just finished a game of travel checkers with Didier. He'd lost. Didier took out a wooden flute and piped a few notes.

"Didier's flute is magic," Daisy said.

Didier frowned. "There's no such thing as magic," he said.

Dillon did not believe this. At least, he didn't want to believe it. There were always things happening that couldn't be explained.

"How do you know?" Dillon asked Didier.

"I just know," said Didier surely. He put the flute to his lips and kept on playing.

Dillon leaned back against the seat. He listened to the musical notes float out the window and dissipate into the air. He was sure they could not possibly finish where his own hearing ended. Maybe there was a land of music. A land where half and whole notes bounced through town, bumping into one another. Dillon smiled at the thought.

"How much longer?" asked Daisy.

"We're almost there," said Dillon's mother.

Didier looked at his watch. "Forty minutes," he said. Daisy began to cry.

"Thanks, Didier," said Dillon's dad.

Dillon closed his eyes. He usually liked riding in the car. Counting the number of trucks they passed. Seeing if he could spot a license plate with the letter *X* on it. But this time was different. Dillon's mind kept wandering. He kept trying to picture the lake in his head. He'd spent every summer of his life there. He ought to know it like the back of his hand. If you'd asked him a week ago, a month ago, he could have pinpointed the location of each tree stump, of each rusty nail in the woodwork. Now that he was on his way there he could not.

He could remember bits and pieces—the wooden cereal bowls piggybacked on the kitchen shelf, the blueberry rake hanging from the wall on the porch, the lime-green bathtub that smelled like pine soap. But he could not re-call what it felt like to step into the water, the waves swallowing his feet, the cold streaming through his body. He couldn't remember the sound of the wooden door, loose on its hinges, or the ribbit of the bullfrogs in the rushes. He couldn't remember the feeling of sunshine clothing him in a blanket of warmth. Last week he could have summoned up all of these things, but now he could not.

Dillon pulled up his knees. There was a rip-ping sound as his moist skin peeled away from the leather seat.

"Daisy's wilting," Didier said loudly. Mrs. Dil-lon turned in her seat. Daisy was as white as chalk.

"Are you feeling sick, Daisy?" she asked. Daisy nodded.

"Did anyone remember the pail?" asked Di-dier.

"Here," said Dillon. He held the sky-blue bucket in front of Daisy and sighed. He'd be making sand castles in that bucket in a couple of days. Dillon was used to this. Daisy usually never made it more than twenty miles from home without throwing up.

"Think of something nice," said Dillon. "Like Disneyland."

Daisy started to cry again.

"Any more good advice, Dill?" asked Didier.

"Open Daisy's window," said Dillon's father.

Dillon reached over and rolled down the window. He put his hands to his ears to block out the sound of Daisy throwing up and looked at the passing cornfields, wondering what tugged them toward the sun. What pulled the clouds across the sky? He knew that science provided a neat set of answers to these questions. But for a moment he preferred to believe it was magic.

Mr. Dillon pulled into the next gas station. "Last stop before Lake Waban," he cried. "Last chance to use the bathroom."

Dillon scrambled out of the car.

"Don't touch the toilet seat," his mother

hollered after him. "And don't forget to wash your hands."

"Okay." Dillon nodded absently. He was used to this too. His mother was a germ trooper, always trying to stamp them out before they got you.

Dillon entered the station. It was like a tiny market. They sold gas, oil, and car parts. But they sold newspapers, music, food, and toys as well. Dillon headed down an aisle and paused before a display of pocket games. He reached in his jacket and found a dollar. Then he chose a bag of tiddlywinks because he liked their colors. He particularly liked the deep sea-green ones. He paid for them and followed the sign to the toilet. There was a line of people waiting.

Dillon studied the tiled walls covered with graffiti. *MARCIA* was written everywhere.

Dillon wondered who Marcia was. What did she look like? What color were her eyes? Was she tall or short? Images of girls he knew passed through Dillon's head. Then his attention turned to the girl standing in front of him. Her hair was wavy brown. It smelled like green apples. She was wearing a shirt with broad blue stripes. It brought back to Dillon a far-off memory of an umbrella somewhere. A large umbrella shielding the sun. The girl was wearing sneakers just like Dillon's with red stripes and grass stains.

"We have the same sneakers," said Dillon. The girl turned around. She looked nice. Very nice.

"Did you say something to me?" she asked.

"It was nothing," said Dillon. "I was just thinking aloud." Dillon knew he shouldn't really talk to this girl. She was a complete stranger. But he wanted to talk to her. He wanted to know where she was going.

"I'm going to Camp Tanglewood," she said. She volunteered the information without even being asked. "It's on Lake Waban."

"I'm going to Lake Waban too," said Dillon. "We have a house there."

"What's your name?" asked the girl. It was the question Dillon always dreaded. But he never lied. He thought you shouldn't lie, especially about a thing like your name.

"Dillon Dillon," said Dillon. He waited for the girl to laugh. To smile in disbelief. To say, "You're kidding." He hoped she wouldn't.

She didn't. "I'm Eunice," she said politely. "Eunice Schroeder."

"How do you spell that?" asked Dillon.

"E-U-N-I-C-E," Eunice pronounced the letters of her name, clearly pausing between each.

"You have the word *nice* in your name," said Dillon. "Did you know that?"

Eunice smiled. She looked at the bag in Dillon's hand. "Are those tiddlywinks?" she asked.

"Yes, they are," said Dillon.

"Great color green," said Eunice.

"I like it too," said Dillon. "In fact green is my favorite color. Blue is a close second," he added.

"Really?" said Eunice. Dillon wondered if she was laughing at him. He hoped she wasn't. Then he reminded himself that he hardly knew her. Why was he telling her something as personal as his favorite color? His friends didn't even know his favorite color.

"Green is my favorite color too," said Eunice, nodding.

Dillon smiled. "Would you like one?" he asked. He held out the bag of tiddlywinks. Eunice took one.

"Thank you," she said.

The line was moving quickly now. Dillon hoped it would slow down, but it didn't. In no time at all, it was Eunice's turn to use the bathroom. Dillon waited for her to finish. Then it was his turn.

"Goodbye, Dillon," she said. "Maybe I'll see you on Lake Waban."

Lake Waban was five miles around. Dillon had never heard of Camp Tanglewood. It was unlikely he'd ever see Eunice again. Still, as he strolled back to the car, he kept hoping that someday Eunice would reappear.

5

IT ALL CAME RUSHING BACK TO DILLON. Just as the car turned off the pavement and headed down a dirt road. Lake Waban was where he'd passed some of the most painful moments of his life. No wonder he'd blocked it out. Learning to swim. Stepping on a nail that had come right up through his big toe. Peeling bloodsuckers from his skin. Dillon flinched as the memories surfaced. Then he sighed as his body flooded with happy recollections too. Memories of twilight barbecues, of birthdays, of famous firsts. First crew cut. First camping trip. First fish. First boat ride. First tree house.

Dillon's father stopped the car. The blinds of

the cottage were down and the windows and doors sealed tight. But the little house smiled out at them all the same, its blue stained clapboards beaming under the sun. Dillon couldn't help but smile back.

Dillon's father stepped out of the car. "Here we are!" he cried. He turned in a circle and took in the nature that surrounded them. He had worked six days a week the entire year to have these two glorious months with no television. No deadlines. No traffic. "To shed the weary hide of winter and grow a new skin," as he put it.

Dillon slid from the car. He and Didier began unloading boxes and bags from the trunk. Wrapping paper, rubber bands, glue, mousetraps, provisions they would probably never need. But Dillon was used to this. This was his mother. She lived by the Scout motto, "Be prepared."

Didier set down a cardboard carton on the kitchen table and groaned. "I hate unpacking," he said. He held up a tube of shoe polish. "Do we really need this?" he asked. "For our sneakers?"

"What if a pair of dress shoes fell from the sky?" teased his mother.

"Shoes don't fall from the sky," said Didier matter-of-factly. Dillon knew he was right. But the idea of shoes tumbling through the clouds, sneakers and pastel-pink sandals tripping through the air, made Dillon feel happy inside.

Didier held up a package of industrial-sized sponges. "What if the lake floods?" he said. Dillon's mother rolled her eyes.

Dillon laughed. What if was a land of endless possibilities. "What if we could fly?" he said. "What if you could see around a corner before even getting there?" Dillon paused. "What if you'd called me David instead of Dillon?" he added, hardly realizing what he had said. But no one had heard, caught up as they were in the notion of what could and what might be.

Dillon finished unloading the car. He wandered out to the lawn.

"Look!" cried Daisy. Dillon looked. Daisy was crouched in a thicket of tall grass and brown-eyed Susans. She cupped a grasshopper in her hand. "It's missing a leg," she said sadly. Dillon leaned forward to look at the bright green bug. Its eye was staring at him. It seemed to be telling him something. Dillon turned away. Now it was Didier's turn.

Didier positioned himself level with the grasshopper. He looked it straight in the eye.

"Hey, fella," he said. He held the knuckle of his finger under the grasshopper's body, so close that its shadow turned his finger green. "Want to get down?" he asked. He did not wait for an answer. "He wants to go," he said to Daisy.

Daisy gently set the grasshopper on a tuft of grass. It hopped off on its one strong leg. But Dillon could still feel its eye like a moonbeam piercing the night. He could not rid himself of the thought that the grasshopper had wanted to say something to him, and he had turned away. Dillon waited for the grasshopper to come back, waited for a second chance, but the grasshopper had moved on. Daisy had moved on too. She was knee-deep in wildflowers, collecting a bouquet of Queen Anne's lace. Didier had begun sorting through a tackle box of fishing flies. And Dillon was stuck in a moment that had already passed.

Dillon watched in wonder as the big shadow of Didier moved across the pale blue wall of the boathouse. It was made even grander by the late afternoon sun. Didier whistled to himself as he sorted the flies by color and size. Without thinking, Dillon began whistling too. That happened sometimes when he was with his friends. Without thinking, Dillon began doing what they did. When Billy Chisholm picked his nose, Dillon's finger found its way to his nostrils. When Simon Jersey cleared his throat and spit on the ground, Dillon coughed up nothing. Didier did not do this. Dillon guessed that was the difference between leaders and followers. Didier was a leader. Dillon was a follower, at least for now. But maybe someday he would be a leader too.

Dillon pushed open the screen door of the cottage. He liked the squeaky sound it made followed by fading claps. So he pushed it again.

"Don't play with the door, Dillon," his mother scolded. She smiled. She often smiled when she told Dillon not to do something. This confused Dillon.

Dillon poured himself a glass of root beer. He couldn't stop thinking about the grasshopper. How it had looked at him. Grasshoppers were lower forms of life. They could not think and reason like people. Still, Dillon could not let go of the idea that the grasshopper knew something that he didn't. That the grasshopper had wanted to talk to him. "Can grasshoppers jump with just one leg?" he asked.

Dillon's mother was not listening. She was rummaging through a shopping bag, searching for sunscreen. "I couldn't have forgotten it," she said.

"Can grasshoppers jump with just one leg?" Dillon asked again.

"I don't know," answered his mother.

"I think they can," said Dillon. He knew they could. He'd just seen it. He'd answered his own question. Then why had he asked? Dillon shrugged. Come to think of it, that was something that happened often too.

"What if grasshoppers were smarter than people?" he said.

"Then I guess they'd be ruling the earth," said his mother.

Dillon imagined himself sitting in the grass with a grasshopper hanging over him. It was explaining why Louis Gottlieb kicked Dillon every time they were in a line together. Why Charlene Aires brought Rice Krispies bars for snack time when she never ate them. And why when Daisy spoke, everyone stopped to listen. It was explaining why on earth anyone would name a child Dillon Dillon.

"Here it is," said Dillon's mother, waving the bottle of sunscreen in the air like a trophy. She called to Daisy and began slathering it on her back. Daisy squirmed and wiggled.

"Stand still," said her mother.

"You don't want a melanoma," said Didier.

"What's a melanoma?" asked Daisy.

"You'll never have to know, honey," said her mother, "if you just stand still and let me put this on you."

Didier turned to Dillon. "How about giving Dad and me a hand with the boat?" he asked. Dillon and Daisy followed him to the boathouse. He and Didier lifted the wooden rowboat from its stand and lugged it down to the shore. Dillon's father handed them the oars.

"Isn't this paradise?" he said.

"Paradise?" teased Didier. "There's no TV."

"And no Cinderella's castle." Daisy frowned. She was remembering Disneyland.

Dillon's father straightened the stern of the boat in the sand and laughed. Dillon's father laughed a lot. Even at things that weren't funny. Or at things that were sad. This confused Dillon. Dillon rested the oars on the floor of the boat.

"Last one in is a rotten egg!" cried Didier. Dillon felt the wake of his brother as he flew past him. Didier raced onto the dock, threw off his T-shirt, and dove into the water. Goose bumps broke out on Dillon's skin.

Didier bobbed to the surface and shook the water from his face.

"C'mon, Captain Courageous," he cried.

"Are you talking to me?" joked Dillon. He knew Didier was talking to him. Dillon waded out to his knees. He dreaded going under, the sensation of being swallowed by the vast and endless cold. He closed his eyes and felt the water rise above his chest. Then he bent backward and floated on the surface, belly to the sun.

"White whale," cried Didier teasingly. Dillon smiled as Daisy's laughter rang out from the shore. He looked down at his stomach. He was pale now, but by summer's end he'd be brown as a berry. They all would.

At six o'clock sharp Mr. O'Leary came out of his cottage across the lake. He strolled out onto his dock and dove in. He'd done this for as long as Dillon could remember. Each day at six o'clock, he swam across the lake and back.

"There's Mr. O'Leary," said Dillon's father. "Sure as the sun rises and sets." Dillon watched him surface. From a distance he looked like a windmill rolling across the water.

"That man is a fish," said Dillon's mother.

"Let me see," squealed Daisy. She strained to see the gills and fins on Mr. O'Leary's back.

"It's just an expression," explained Didier.

"Is it?" said Dillon, who had wandered aimlessly back into the land of endless possibilities. Could a man become a fish? He didn't see why not. Caterpillars turned into butterflies.

Suddenly Dillon's eye was caught by an umbrella with blue stripes fluttering in the breeze. He was reminded of the filling station and Eunice Schroeder.

"Has anyone ever heard of Camp Tanglewood?" he asked. No one answered.

"It's a summer camp," added Dillon. "And it's on this lake."

"You have to do better than that," said Dillon's father. "There must be half a dozen summer camps on this lake."

Dillon couldn't do better than that. That's all he knew. Camp Tanglewood was somewhere on this lake and Eunice Schroeder was there. That could be her bubble-gum wrapper that had washed onto the shore right in front of him. But no, thought Dillon, Eunice did not look like a litterbug. Dillon reached down. He picked up the wrapper and put it in his pocket.

At bedtime Dillon was still thinking about Camp Tanglewood.

"Who's sleeping where?" asked Dillon's mother.

"I'm taking the bed on the porch," announced Didier.

"You are?" asked Dillon.

"What's wrong with the porch?" asked Didier.

"Nothing," said Dillon. But that's not what he was thinking. The porch was glassed in, a door flanked by a wall of windows. It was close to the sounds of night. In the bed on the porch, the lake's reflection shone in on you. The cottage lamps unmasked your sleeping face. The fireflies hovered outside like tiny flashlights seeking you out. You were exposed. You were alone. That's what was wrong with the bed on the porch. But Dillon didn't say so.

He couldn't tell Didier the truth. But at least he could tell it to himself. He and Didier had always slept together in the loft above the porch. They had felt each other's breath and listened to each other toss and turn under the covers. They whispered secrets, secrets that would never find their way out of the blackness of the room.

Now Didier was claiming the bed on the porch for his own. What did that mean?

"I'll sleep with Dillon," cried Daisy. Daisy had always slept on a cot in the same room with her parents.

"The loft's for the guys," said Dillon, trying to sound tough. He did not feel tough. He felt abandoned by Didier.

"Can't I sleep with Dillon?" asked Daisy.

"No," said Dillon.

"Dillon," said his mother. "Put yourself in Daisy's shoes."

Dillon lay awake a long time. He searched the dark for the feeling he'd lost. The feeling of Didier lying next to him. Then he got up and peeked through the small oval window above his bed. The lake stretched on endlessly, etched in moonlight. From its center rose an island bathed in blackness. Could it be that Dillon had never noticed it before? Islands didn't grow overnight. That island must have been there for as long as Dillon had. Even longer.

Dillon turned to Daisy. She looked like an angel curled up in bed with her hair spread across the pillow. Her breathing was faster than Didier's. "Put yourself in Daisy's shoes." That's what Dillon's mother had said. Sure, it was just an expression. Like Mr. O'Leary being a fish. The world was full of expressions. "Don't count your chickens before they hatch." "Row your own boat." Those were favorites of Ms. Ryan, Dillon's teacher. Dillon repeated them to the walls.

Suddenly he was aware that he was talking to himself. And someone was talking back. At least, it seemed that way. Each time Dillon spoke, a loon called mournfully from across the lake. The echo of its voice seemed to travel through the walls, into Dillon's bones, to the very depths of his soul.

Dillon was not sure why he did what he did

next. He only knew that he couldn't help himself. Without thinking, he walked over to Daisy's pink quilted slippers, which lay on the floor beneath the bed.

"Put yourself in Daisy's shoes," he whispered. Then he pushed his feet into the tiny quilted chambers. They were small and tight. Dillon was glad no one could see him. He stepped forward, slid backward, then scuffed across the floor. Daisy turned in her sleep. Dillon paused. Then he crept down the stairs. Didier was breathing peacefully in the square bed on the porch. He'd thrown the covers off and was exposed to all the world. Dillon yearned to be swept up into Didier's courage. When he started back up the stairs, a thread from the slipper caught around his baby toe and he wished that Didier would be pulled back to the loft on this same thread. Dillon sighed. In his own shoes, he had felt a longing to be with a big brother. But in Daisy's shoes, he felt it even more.

Dillon placed the slippers back under Daisy's bed. He fell asleep, but every so often he awoke, summoned by the gentle trill of the loon. As the shades of night lifted and day filtered in, Dillon was drawn again to the window, to the island.

He could not lose the feeling that the island was watching him just like the eye of the grasshopper.

In the morning Didier's bed was empty. Dillon was sure he'd been kidnapped or taken by a wood sprite.

"Didier's gone," he said. His parents did not seem worried.

"Didier's out on the lake fishing," said his father.

Dillon looked across the water. He could just make out the shape of Didier bent over in the rowboat cradled by the morning waves. For the first time it occurred to Dillon that this year was not like years past when he and Didier had collected worms and stood on the dock fishing for perch. When they'd lain lost in the tall grass studying crickets and June bugs.

Dillon's father headed for the dock.

"Come on down," he called to Dillon. But Dillon held back, a quiet observer stung by the knowledge that Didier had rolled out of a cocoon and he, Dillon, had yet to be bound.

6

JUNE 21. The first day of summer. The first day of Dillon's life. It was Dillon's birthday. He was ten.

Dillon strolled to the mailbox, a metal cage on a wooden post, at the end of the dirt road. He turned his face upward to the sun. All of life seemed to gravitate toward its warmth and light. The raspberries ripening on their vines. The grass with its long tapered points. The rocky ledges that rose out of the field, their backs clothed in lichen.

The red flag was down. That meant the mailman had come. Dillon reached for the bundle. Lying between the layers of newspaper was a birthday card from Dillon's grandmother. She lived in France and Dillon only saw her every two years, but she always remembered his birthday. Dillon read the card. "Have a Hot Dog of a Birthday" it said. When he opened it, a ten-dollar bill was tucked in its fold and a giant wiener with a smiling face jumped out at him. It was silly, even dumb, but Dillon laughed all the same. He opened and closed the card several times. Then he stuffed it in his shirt pocket and started back down the dirt road.

Dillon's mother had set the picnic table with bright green plates and napkins. Dillon sat down. His place was at the head of the table. He squirted mustard onto a hot dog and spread it with a finger. Daisy watched him admiringly.

"Would you mind using some silverware?" said Dillon's mother. Dillon picked up a knife.

"What do you want to be when you grow up, Dillon?" Daisy asked.

Dillon groaned. He hated that question. "I don't know," he said. The truth was that he hadn't given it much thought. But Dillon didn't tell the truth. "I could be a teacher," he said. Then the image of a garbage truck popped into

Dillon's head. "Or a garbage collector," he added.

"Nobody wants to be a garbage collector," said Didier with his usual air of authority. "Who wants to smell trash all day?"

"Someone has to do it," said Dillon's father.

Dillon recalled the deep green of the garbage truck back home. The grinding and thumping noises as it swallowed the trash, sucked up the garbage cans, sterilized them, and spit them back out. Strangely enough, he hadn't thought of the smell.

"Somebody might want to be a garbage collector," Dillon said slowly. He wondered if he really might want to do that. There was something very satisfying about cleaning up. And he was sure he could do it well.

"I'm going to be a painter," said Daisy. Dillon's mother was a painter. She painted rock walls on canvas and gave them names.

"Good for you," said Dillon, who had begun slowly ticking off in his head the things he would *not* be. He would not be an artist like his mother. Nor would he be a professional thinker like his dad. Dillon's father worked for a government think tank. He was actually paid to sit in an office all day and come up with ideas. Dillon was sure he would not do that.

"Can we change the subject?" he asked.

"Dillon doesn't know what he wants to be," said Daisy.

"Yes I do," said Dillon, who hadn't the least idea. He eyed Didier's fishing reel leaning against the boathouse wall. "I want to be a fisherman," he said.

"Really?" said Dillon's father. He looked amused.

"Way to go," said Didier.

"Dillon's going to be a fisherman," said Daisy, finally satisfied.

Dillon's mother brought out the cake. Dillon stared down at the mounds of icing, which looked like whitecaps on the sea, and the ten yellow candles blazing like half moons. He looked at his parents, their faces stretched with emotion, and he saw what he'd known all along. They *couldn't* have named him Dillon Dillon. Not on purpose.

"Happy birthday to you," Dillon's mother

sang out. The others joined in and Dillon blushed bashfully.

"Make a wish!" shouted Daisy. Dillon never knew what to wish for. Usually he blew out the candles before he could think of something. This year was no different.

Didier shoved an odd-shaped package at Dillon. It was wrapped in brown paper and bound with fishing line. "Open it, Dill," he said.

Dillon had spent the week hoping for things he knew he wouldn't get: a dog, his own rowboat, or a ten-speed bike. And hoping not to get things that were likely: a ski sweater, a magazine subscription to *National Geographic*, new underwear and socks.

Dillon tore the paper from Didier's gift. Inside was a boomerang. Dillon took hold of it. He stroked its smooth wooden surface and felt its graceful bend.

"It's a boomerang," said Daisy. "If you throw it, it comes back to you."

"You have to throw it properly," added Didier. He took the boomerang in his strong arm and sent it skyward. It spun laughingly in circles. Then suddenly it turned on its elbow, cutting the air, and landed at Dillon's feet.

"Amazing," said Dillon. "How does it do that?"

"That's its destiny," said Dillon's father. "Always to return to the thrower."

"Let me try," said Dillon. He sent the boomerang flying, but it flip-flopped onto the ground.

"It'll come," said his father. "Give it time."

"Open my present," cried Daisy. She stuck a small square box under Dillon's nose. "It's a watch," she said.

Didier covered Daisy's mouth. "You're not supposed to tell," he said.

"Oops," said Daisy.

"It's okay, Daisy," said Dillon. He pulled the wrapping from the box. Inside was a green-and-blue water-resistant watch with a magnifying glass over the date. June 21.

"Thanks," Dillon said to Daisy. "It's just what I've always wanted." Dillon wrapped the watch around his wrist. Its rhythmic tick seemed to set the world in motion.

"Do you like it?" asked Daisy.

"I love it," said Dillon, awash with happiness. He hoped the feeling would last forever.

The phone rang. Dillon's father answered it.

"It's for you, Dillon," he called. "It's Papa." Papa was Dillon's father's father.

Dillon went into the house. He took the receiver. "Hi, Grandpa," he said.

"Happy birthday," drawled Dillon's grandfather. Dillon had a hard time deciphering what he was saying. He was from the Deep South, and each word he uttered sounded as if it had been flattened by a rolling pin.

"Ten years old," he said. "Attaboy." Dillon shrugged. He hadn't done anything special to become ten. It had come to him.

"Happens to us all," said Dillon, fidgeting with the phone cord. He felt embarrassed.

"How's Hairy?" asked Grandpa.

Hairy was their dog. He'd died three years ago, right after Dillon's grandmother. But Dillon's grandfather had forgotten.

"He's dead, Grandpa. Remember?" said Dillon.

"God rest his soul," said Grandpa. "I've sent you a compass for your birthday," he added. "So you won't get lost." He chuckled heartily.

"Just what I need," said Dillon politely.

"Well, I'd better let you go," said his grandfather. "You ten-year-olds have a lot to do."

"Thanks for calling," said Dillon. He handed the phone to his father.

"Our present is down at the shore," said Dillon's mother. Daisy grabbed Dillon's hand and pulled him across the lawn toward the lake. On the shore around the bend, sparkling under the midday sun, was a boat. A red rowboat. On its stern painted in ivory-colored letters were the words *Dillon Dillon*. The bold letters of his name beamed out at Dillon. On a math paper in Ms. Ryan's fourth-grade class, that name held no weight. But displayed on the broad red surface of a boat, it had something almost magnificent about it.

"Is that for me?" Dillon asked, unbelieving.

"It sure is," said Dillon's mother.

"I don't know any other Dillon Dillon," said his father.

Dillon walked over to the boat. He ran his hand along the solid red frame. He and Didier had always shared a boat, the boat that Didier trolled in. But last year Didier had painted it a mustard yellow and mounted the words *Sting Ray* on its side. Then he'd gotten a small outboard motor, and slowly but surely the boat had slipped from Dillon's grasp. Now Dillon had a boat of his own.

Daisy clambered in and perched herself on the narrow wooden seat of the bow.

"The truth is, we ordered a green boat, but the guy who took the order made a mistake, and this is what arrived," said Dillon's dad.

"The truth is, I wish it were mine," said Didier, smiling gently and rubbing the boat's stern with the palm of his hand.

It was a day of truths. A day when the clouds retreated and the sun came out of hiding. A day when the dragonflies hovered shamelessly, waiting for their prey. Dillon looked at his parents. Both of them. And he decided that he too would join in the spirit of honesty which nature flaunted that day.

"Why did you name me Dillon Dillon?" he asked all at once.

Dillon's father paused. He coughed nervously. "It's a long story," he said.

"How long?" asked Dillon. He looked at his watch, the one Daisy had just given him. He had no plans. He had the entire day. The one after as well. He had two and a half months before he had to be back at school. "Why would anybody name a child Dillon Dillon?" he said.

He turned to his mother. "This was not how it was supposed to happen," she said. She had been preparing for this moment for years, carefully measuring words and storing them in the same way that she stashed shoe polish, pins, Band-Aids, glue. Now she was speechless. "Do you want to begin, Sam?" she asked.

Dillon's father reached his arm around Dillon's shoulders and drew him near. He beckoned to Didier and Daisy, and they were all pulled together in a loose circle.

Even before his father had spoken, Dillon could feel truth with a capital *T* hurtling toward him at the speed of light. But Dillon knew there was no turning back.

"We didn't name you Dillon Dillon," said his father. "Not exactly, anyway."

Dillon's father gazed at the sand. He shifted his feet, sifting through the blue-and-gray flecks of crushed shell and gravel.

"The truth is, Dillon, we're not your first parents," he said.

"What?" said Dillon, feeling suspended in

space, not knowing which way to turn. Not knowing where home was.

"You were my sister Maggie's little boy," continued his father. He did not look at Dillon as he spoke, his gaze settling on some faraway place and time. "You were her baby," he said.

Dillon turned back to his mother. She looked as though she might cry. Dillon hoped she wouldn't.

"Maggie named you Dillon after her family," she said. "You were Dillon McDermott. McDermott was your father's family name. Then, when you were eighteen months old, Maggie and your father died in a plane accident and you came to us." Dillon's mother paused. She took a deep breath and continued. "We adopted you and gave you our family name. Dillon. Like Didier and Daisy. We could have changed your first name. But we didn't. It just didn't seem right after eighteen months," she said. "We already knew and loved you as Dillon."

"So you became Dillon Dillon," said his father. He coughed again nervously.

Dillon leaned into the rowboat. He had never heard of anything so absurd. He knew that his father's sister and her husband had died in a plane accident. But he did not know they had any children. And now to think that they were his parents. And these two people in front of him were only fill-ins. Dillon looked at his watch. He was sorry he'd turned ten. He was sorry time had moved ahead and brought him to this knowledge.

"It shouldn't have had to happen this way," said Dillon's mother again. "You shouldn't have had to ask."

Why hadn't they told him before, thought Dillon.

His mother read his mind. "We wanted to tell you, Dillon," she said. "Seven seemed like a good age. You were old enough to understand. Then Grandma got sick. She died and we put it off. When you were eight we moved and you started a new school. It didn't seem right to tell you then." Dillon's mother placed her hand on the back of his neck. "I'm sorry it's come to this," she said.

"Time flies, Dillon," said his father. Then he added, "I know that's no excuse."

Dillon was silent for a moment. Then he spoke. "McDermott." He repeated that other name out loud.

"You remember Mamie?" said Dillon's mother.

Dillon did remember Mamie. Mamie was like family to them. Dillon used to visit her in that tall high-rise in the city. She'd had a desk loaded with Life Savers for him and Daisy and Didier. And she never forgot a birthday or Christmas. Images bobbed to the surface of Dillon's consciousness. Mamie whose bright blue watery eyes seemed always on the verge of brimming over. Mamie who always said how much Dillon reminded her of his father. Mamie who had had three husbands. Mamie who was now in a nursing home.

"Mamie is your father's mother," said Dillon's father. "We don't know which of her husbands was your grandfather."

"Mamie is my grandmother," said Dillon. "And I have a grandpa I never knew."

"None of us knew him," said Dillon's mother.

Dillon sighed deeply. So life and circumstance had conspired to keep this knowledge from him. Well, that explained why Daisy and Didier were tongue rollers and he wasn't. They could stick out their tongues and roll them into a log. Dillon's tongue lay flat in his mouth no matter how much he twisted and turned it. Still, Dillon had hoped that if he kept practicing, one day he too would become a tongue roller. Now he knew that would never happen. His real parents must not have been tongue rollers. Dillon looked down at his feet, the sneakers with the air-cushioned soles. And at that moment he wished to be in anyone else's shoes.

"It's not true," said Dillon, quietly hoping. But he knew in his heart that it was.

Dillon looked for Daisy, who had strayed off in search of blueberries. She had not been listening. Or she was too small to understand. Didier was leaning against a tree clutching his fishing pole. He did not know what to say.

"Say something, Dillon," said his father.

"So Daisy and Didier aren't really my brother and sister," said Dillon.

"But they are," said Dillon's mother.

"They're my cousins," said Dillon flatly. How strange this sounded. Dillon thought that he had no cousins. His mother's brothers had no children, and Dillon's father had had just one sister.

Dillon got to his feet and turned away from his family. He could no longer bear watching his parents squirm before him. Or the feeling that

Didier and Daisy had been lifted by the wind and carried away.

Off to Dillon's right the striped umbrella wavered from its perch in the sand. It reminded Dillon of Eunice Schroeder's shirt glowing under the fluorescent lights of the gas station. She was here, somewhere on this great lake. Dillon had not made a birthday wish. He had not been able to think of anything. Now a dozen wishes passed through his head, none of which were likely to come true.

7

"ARE YOU ALL RIGHT?" asked Dillon's mother. "Do you want to talk?"

"I'm okay," Dillon lied. But he was not okay. How could he be?

"Please look at me, Dillon," said his mother. But Dillon would not look. He didn't want to be reminded that they were not even related by blood. That they had not shared that lifeline which he'd learned about in science class. That the same splash of freckles across each cheek, the same way of wrinkling up their noses against the sunlight, the same habit of nibbling on their thumbs were simple coincidences.

All at once it dawned on Dillon. For his entire

life he had felt something was missing. Something was wrong. Now he knew what that was. And as it began to sink deeper into his being, it hurt.

"Do you want to shell peas with me?" asked Dillon's mother. Dillon usually liked shelling peas. Pinching the swollen sides of the bright green pods. Listening to the snap as they opened. Touching their soft velvet beds.

"No," said Dillon.

"Want a piece of candy?" asked Daisy, shoving a lollipop under Dillon's nose.

"No," said Dillon loudly.

"You don't need to shout," said Dillon's mother. "We're standing right next to you."

But Dillon did need to shout. He needed to scream and to stamp his feet.

Dillon wandered down to the shore. He waded out among the cattails. Their soft brown backs brushed against his skin.

"Ribbit," he called. A bullfrog croaked back. Dillon closed his eyes. "Ribbit, ribbit," he cried loudly again and again. Then he opened his eyes. Swimming toward him was a bird. A loon. Dillon didn't notice its black-and-white feathers. He noticed its small red eye. An eye just like that of the grasshopper, which looked straight at Dillon as though it had something to say.

"Ribbit," said Dillon softly. The loon called back. Three times it called back. Then it cocked its head and disappeared below the surface of the water.

"Wait," cried Dillon. Seconds later the loon resurfaced. But when Dillon spoke again, the loon was silent.

"Please talk," Dillon begged. He sounded like his mother now. But the loon would not speak. It swam in circles, pitching its head from side to side. Finally it swam off. But in the gentle swash of its wake Dillon thought he could hear his name. "Dillon, Dillon. Oh, Dillon."

That night Daisy slept with her parents. Didier returned to the loft.

"You don't have to sleep with me," said Dillon.

"I know," said Didier. He browsed the bookshelf and pulled out a book on fly-fishing. Didier was convinced that if he slept with the book under his pillow he could assimilate the contents without actually reading them. That the ideas would simply seep into his head as he dreamed. "Heads are porous," he explained.

"What's porous?" asked Dillon. Didier did not answer.

Dillon's father came up the stairs. He kissed Didier's, then Dillon's forehead, and turned out the light. Then he lingered in the shadows a little longer than usual before heading back down.

After a while Didier spoke. "How are you doing, Dill?" he asked.

"I'm okay," said Dillon. He turned to Didier, whose strong, handsome profile glowed in the moonlight.

"It's a bummer, Dill," said Didier. He slid his tongue along his lower lip.

Dillon began to do the same. Then he stopped himself.

"But it doesn't change anything," added Didier.

"I know," said Dillon. But he did not believe it. Knowing and believing were two different things.

"I remember when you came to us," said Didier. "I must have been about four. They said you were a gift and I believed it. I still do," he whispered as he turned toward the wall.

Dillon waited for Didier to fall asleep. He willed himself to listen. He longed to hear their breath in unison, woven in a nocturnal lullaby as it used to be. Instead, from far across the lake a loon called, a strange and mysterious cry that spiraled through the night. Dillon remembered the loon he had seen earlier that day. Its red eye, its voice. The more Dillon tried to listen for Didier's breathing, the louder he heard the wail of the loon. Dillon rose from his bed. He went to the window. The island was there beckoning him as before, and in the background the cry of the loon. It sounded as though it was laughing and crying at once. As though it was speaking and calling to him. "Dillon Dillon, Dillon Dillon, dill pickle, daffy-down dilly . . ."

8

Wherever the loon exists there are many stories,
mystical and magical. In some, loon becomes a man.
In others, man becomes a loon. In all, the distinction
between man and animal has melted away to reveal
the loon's magical power to take us back to who and
what we are . . .

DILLON WOKE EARLY. He had not slept with a
book under his pillow. Nonetheless, a cluster of
discomforting thoughts had flowered in the
night. Could parents who adopt a child love
him as much as the two who are their own? Especially when one is a ray of sunshine and the
other is Didier? What else had his parents not

told him? These questions were a wild tangle in Dillon's head.

Dillon crept quietly down to the kitchen. He stopped in front of the wooden bowls stacked one on top of the other. All that had seemed clear and known yesterday seemed fuzzy today. Dillon poured himself a bowl of Rice Krispies. He listened to the snap, crackle, pop of the cereal bursting in milk. It was a comforting sound. Then he pulled out a chair and sat down to eat. Automatically, he filled out the coupon on the back of the cereal box. He could win a mountain bike or a new stereo system. Dillon did not want either, but he filled out the coupon just the same. When he was finished, Dillon washed his bowl. An empty coffee mug sat on the table. It belonged to Dillon's father. Dillon picked it up and rinsed that too. Then he set them side by side in the dish rack to dry.

Dillon turned toward the window. The sun had just risen. Its rays sliced through the still lake like lightning bolts. Dillon's father was down at the shore. He stood leaning to the right in a thinker's pose. Dillon had always wondered where his father got his ideas. Now it occurred to him that maybe it was somewhere in these quiet dawns with their vague stirrings of life that his ideas came to him. Perhaps on a wave, a breeze, or a beam of sunlight.

Dillon strapped his new watch tightly to his wrist. He tucked his boomerang into his belt and headed down to the shore. His rowboat was waiting, his name glowing in the sun. Dillon walked over to it.

"You're up early," said his father.

Dillon shrugged. He gripped the stern of the boat and gave it a gentle push into the water. "I thought I'd try her out," he said.

Dillon's father laughed uncomfortably. "Any idea where?" he asked.

"What about back in time?" said Dillon.

Dillon's father curled his lip. It fell somewhere between a laugh and a frown. "I wish I knew the way," he said.

Dillon took his place in the stern of the boat and slid the oars into the oarlocks. Straight ahead was the island. It looked different in broad daylight. Sureness and clarity had replaced the eerie shadows and made last night's vision seem all a dream. Still Dillon felt the tug of memory call to him. And he knew he had to go.

"I'm going to the island," he said.

"Good choice," said Dillon's father. Dillon looked into his face. It was pinched and unsettled. Something inside of Dillon moved like water tumbling over a fall.

"Do you want to come?" he asked. He hoped his father would say yes.

"Why not," said his father. He climbed aboard and seated himself in the bow. Dillon grabbed the oars and began to row. He listened to the squeak of the blades as they displaced water into tiny orbs. When he glanced back toward the cottage, he saw his mother standing on the lawn waving. She was no more than one hundred feet away, but it felt like a lifetime.

After a while Dillon dropped the oars. He let the boat drift. He could see clear to the bottom of the lake, the sandy rolling underwater hills, the shuddering plant life wakened by the sun streaming through. Hovering over him like a guardian angel was his father's reflection.

"Penny for your thoughts," said his father.

Dillon squinted. On the shore the beach umbrella fluttered in the wind, an ongoing tribute to Eunice Schroeder. "I was thinking about Eunice," he answered honestly. "Eunice Schroeder."

"Who's Eunice Schroeder?" asked his father.

"Someone I met," answered Dillon. "Someone nice," he added.

"Where did you meet her?" asked his father.

"At the gas station," answered Dillon.

"Eunice," said his father. "I like that name. Eunice," he said again.

"Eunice," repeated Dillon.

"Dillon," said Dillon's father.

"Dillon, Dillon," said Dillon. "Dillon, Dillon, Dillon, Dillon, Dillon." He paused. "You know you could have changed my name," he whispered. "I wouldn't have minded."

"You might even have liked it," said Dillon's father.

Dillon blushed.

"You see, Dillon, it's hard to explain why people do certain things," his father continued. "At the time it seemed right." He took a deep breath, then went on. "Your name was something your parents had given you. Dillon was who you were. And Dillon is who we are. So it just seemed right."

Dillon's father fumbled in his back pocket. He pulled out his wallet. Hidden in a small compartment was a picture. He handed it to Dillon. "Here they are," he said.

Dillon studied the photo. Two people smiled out at him, tanned and happy, from a sandy beach. A tall lanky man and a woman with long wavy hair. Dillon thought he had seen them before. Maybe he had in baby pictures, in family photos. But he'd never really looked at them, not like he did now.

"He was big," said Dillon.

"He was," said his father. "His name was Jon."

"Jon," repeated Dillon, striving to feel some connection. Straining to see if these two people were in some small visible way like him. He didn't see himself in either. Different hair, different eyes, different everything. They were where Dillon's life had begun. Yet they were strangers.

"Where are they now?" asked Dillon.

"Their stones are in a cemetery," answered Dillon's father. "But they're buried at the bottom of the sea."

Dillon bit his lip and nodded.

"I wish I knew more, Dillon," said his father. "But no one really knows what happens after death."

"I know that," said Dillon. He had never really thought much about dying. But now he found himself thinking about heaven. And he found himself harboring a secret wish that the sky were a one-way mirror and that Maggie and Jon were looking down on him.

Dillon turned the photo over in his hand.

"Keep it," said his father. He picked up the oars and began rowing. Dillon tucked the picture in his shirt pocket. He thought of the dozens of gum wrappers and baseball cards that had ended up in the washing machine, and he hoped he would remember to take it out.

Dillon's eyes moved across the floor of the boat to his father's shoes. Brown leather with blue rubber soles. Dillon counted the rivets and the airholes in their sides. It was funny how shoes could breathe, how they had tongues. Just like people. Dillon looked at his own sneakers. They had cushioned soles that bounced up and down with each step. Dillon wiggled his toes. He remembered the feel of Daisy's slippers. "Put yourself in Daisy's shoes," his mother had said. And suddenly Dillon was overcome with a peculiar longing.

"Can I try on one of your shoes?" he asked his father.

Dillon's father kicked off a shoe. "Be my guest," he said. Dillon untied his sneaker and stepped into his father's boat shoe. It was warm. He could feel the hills and slopes carved out by his father's foot. The spaces rubbed soft from use. He wondered in which part of the shoe he would feel the loss of a sister. Or Dillon's own sudden entrance into his life.

"So how does it feel?" asked his father.

"Big," said Dillon, stretching his toes toward the tip.

Dillon's father laughed. "Someday you'll fill it out," he said.

Dillon did not notice the island until they had been scooped up into its shadow.

Dillon's father pulled in the oars and held the boat while Dillon stepped onto land and tied the boat to a tree.

"I used to come here when I was a boy," said his father. "I used to imagine that I was a conqueror or a pirate. That this was a magical place. A place where anything could happen."

Dillon followed his father over rough patches of lichen washed to a faded blue. Below his feet shells, snails, and driftwood were woven into an exquisite tapestry. Dillon's father knelt down next to the roots of a pine tree. "I buried three silver dollars here once," he said. "I came back to dig them up, but I never found them."

Dillon waited for his father to continue, but he was interrupted by a cry that seemed to come from the very core of the island. It was the same sound that had wakened Dillon the night before. The same rolling laughter that seemed to say, "Dillon Dillon, Dillon Dillon."

"Listen," said Dillon's father. "A loon."

Dillon listened as the sound burst forth anew. "What is it saying?" he asked.

"I don't know. You'll have to ask it," answered his father.

Dillon wove in and out among the bushes. Each time he was sure where the cry was coming from, it changed. Dillon neared the end of the island. The course that Mr. O'Leary swam each day shimmered like a golden pathway on the surface of the water. In its wake was the loon sitting motionless. Around its neck water droplets shone like jewels. It was the same loon Dillon had seen the day before.

"It's you again," said Dillon. No sooner had Dillon spoken than the loon disappeared beneath the waves. Dillon waited. He held his breath and stood perfectly still, but the loon did not reappear.

"It's playing hide-and-seek," said Dillon's father. Seconds later Dillon heard a sharp cry. He moved toward the sound, but now it was in back of him. Dillon hid himself in a clump of bushes. He stayed for a long time. A fleet of dragonflies and a flurry of blackflies dared to show themselves. But not the loon. Every so often it hooted and laughed, but it would not come out.

At last a strange and mysterious silence settled. The game was over. The loon had ceased to call.

"It's gone," said Dillon. He stood perfectly still in the middle of the island, in a bubble of peace. He wished he could stay there forever.

"Don't worry," said Dillon's father. "It'll be back."

"I hope so," whispered Dillon, not able to shake the feeling that something was happening to him. Something deep within, undetectable to the naked eye.

9

The call of the loon is its own language, understood not just by its own kind but by other creatures too. It is the language not just of mind, but of mind and heart . . .

DILLON LAY IN BED. Didier lay next to him reading a book on fly-fishing. He opened to chapter three. It was all about knots. Nail knots, needle knots, arbor knots. Didier studied the diagrams, carefully tracing each step with his finger.

Dillon reached for his shirt, which hung on the back of a chair, and pulled the picture of his parents out of the pocket. He had felt it there all afternoon, though it weighed nothing. Now he turned the photo over in his hands. He had hoped to feel love for those two smiling faces. But as darkness settled, the outlines of the people faded until Dillon could no longer make them out clearly. All chances of feeling them were gone. Dillon put the picture under his pillow and turned to Didier.

"Mind if I turn off the light?" he asked.

"Go ahead," said Didier. Dillon flicked the switch on the wall. They lay in blackness for a long time. Only then did Dillon dare think of that other life that could have been if only . . .

If only his real parents had not died. Dillon would have been the first. He might have been a big brother, sure and strong. Or he might have been an only child. He would have had cousins. Didier and Daisy. But he wouldn't have known them as he did now, the shading of their voices, the rhythms of their breath. He would have had another name. Dillon McDermott. Dillon imagined it scribbled at the top of his math paper. He would have been a different person. In the quiet, Dillon conjured up a boy he hardly knew, surrounded by shadow and mystery. And it dawned on him how important those ifs and if nots really were.

At last the silence was broken. Off in the distance a loon laughed gloriously. Dillon spoke.

"Did you hear that?" he asked.

"Hear what?" answered Didier.

"The loon," said Dillon. "I think it's saying *Dillon*."

"Loons can't say *Dillon*," Didier said.

"What are they saying, then?" asked Dillon.

"Loons can't talk," said Didier.

"But what if they could?" said Dillon. "What if they were calling me?"

Didier sighed impatiently. "Why would they be calling you? What would they have to tell you?" he said.

"I don't know," said Dillon. Dillon did not know. But he fell asleep thinking of feathers, birds, flying. Tomorrow he would return to the island and maybe he would find out. Meanwhile he would hope. Hope that as he slept the loon's secret message might seep into his head like the knowledge that Didier stored under his pillow.

10

DIDIER BAITED HIS CRAYFISH POTS and piled them into his boat. "It's going to be a scorcher," he said.

Dillon was preparing his own boat. He already felt sticky with heat and it was barely eight o'clock.

Dillon's mother handed him a sandwich, a thermos of water, and a tube of sunscreen. "Home for lunch," she said. Dillon did not know if it was a question or a command. He guessed it was a command, and he nodded before pushing off.

Dillon gripped the oars and headed toward the island. He rowed effortlessly. The assault of heat had caused a great retreat of life. The bull-frogs had ceased ribbiting in the rushes. Not even the trees stirred. Dillon gazed at the clouds, which looked like sheep's wool tacked to the sky. He scanned the shore, hoping to catch a glimpse of Camp Tanglewood.

At last Dillon stepped onto the island and tied the boat to a tree. He wandered to the spot where his father had buried the three coins, and knelt down. He began to dig. If he kept at it long enough, he was sure he would find the three silver dollars. Dillon dug for what seemed like forever, turning back layers of earth and layers of feeling. He felt happiness, then sadness, fear, and courage all mingled together in the tiers of dirt. Still, there were no coins, and what finally settled around Dillon was loneliness. It was a strange feeling. But it did not last long.

The loon had returned and was nearing the edge of the island, preening its black-and-white feathers. It seemed not to notice Dillon. But as Dillon watched it, an odd feeling overcame him. A sound moved through his body and traveled to his mouth. It popped out like a small shriek, startling the bird. The loon looked up at Dillon. Straight into his eyes. Dillon remembered the grasshopper. He remembered his mother. And this time he looked back.

"Hi there," said Dillon.

The loon laughed.

"What's so funny?" asked Dillon.

The bird let out a hoot, which startled Dillon. Then it closed its sharp beak firmly. Dillon longed to reach out and touch it, to feel the feathers that looked like woven ink. He held out his hand.

"Here, peeper," he said.

The loon did not hesitate. It climbed awkwardly onto the island, moving upright one foot at a time. Then it flopped, and slid along on its belly like a seal.

"I'm Dillon," Dillon said. "Dillon Dillon. Dillon Dillon Dillon Dillon Dillon Dillon." He waited for the loon to laugh.

The loon opened its mouth. But it did not laugh. It shook its feathers and its head in a frenzy of movement. Then it pecked Dillon gently right on the soft part of his hand between his thumb and forefinger. Dillon stood up and stepped back.

"What was that for?" he asked. The loon did not answer. With its beak it began digging in the dirt under its feet, collecting debris in its mouth. Then it began piling twigs and moss on Dillon's left foot.

"What are you doing?" cried Dillon. "That's my sneaker."

The loon kept right on digging, and piling. When Dillon tried to pull his foot away, the loon hooted loudly. It stopped and stared at Dillon with a red eye that seemed bottomless.

"All right," said Dillon. He crouched down, unlaced his sneaker, and carefully pulled his foot out of it. "Have it your way," he said. "But I'm warning you it probably stinks."

The loon stuck its beak into the sneaker. Then it balanced on the edge of the shoe. It did not seem to care if Dillon's shoe stank or not.

Dillon sank his bare foot into the surrounding moss. It felt squishy and nice. Had he never stepped on moss before? Dillon walked in a small circle. He felt the hardness of rocks, the roughness of lichen, the smoothness of stones, the frailness of twigs breaking under him. It was as though his foot had been asleep forever and had just awoken.

Dillon removed his other sneaker. "I'm keeping this one," he said to the loon, who was now amassing dried leaves and cattails and dragging them toward the sneaker.

Dillon felt hungry. He reached into his backpack and pulled out a sandwich.

"Want some?" he asked, offering a bite to the loon. "It's ham and cheese." The loon pecked at the bread. Dillon laid a piece on the ground. The loon pecked at it again. Then it put the crust in the sneaker.

Dillon picked up a soggy pinecone. He tossed it to the loon. The loon took it in its beak and added it to the pile. Then it started hobbling around the sneaker, hopping from one foot to the other. Dillon got up and began hopping too. He'd never done anything that silly before. Except talk to a bird. He'd been talking to a bird. And now he was dancing with one. Dillon hoped no one was watching.

Suddenly the loon moved closer to Dillon. Dillon was sure it would speak. Instead it gave Dillon another peck on the hand. A gentle peck, warm and wet. Afterward it lapsed into silence and began preening its feathers.

"Are you trying to tell me something?" asked Dillon.

The loon paid him no attention. It continued

its quest for leaves and twigs and began placing them around Dillon's left sneaker.

Dillon did not get it. "What are you doing?" he asked, reaching his hand toward the loon. He got one last peck before the loon took to the water and disappeared.

Dillon put his right sneaker back on. He glanced back at the other one, a monument ensconced in moss and twigs, and shrugged to himself. As he climbed into his boat he realized that his hand was tingling. He held it up to the light. It looked no different but it felt different.

Dillon drifted for a while, hoping to see the loon's head bob to the surface. But it did not.

At last Dillon picked up his oars and rowed the long stretch toward shore. He hoped no one would notice his missing sneaker.

11

Once a boy was called upon to create a bird. The boy asked Creator to color the loon in shades of gray. After, when Creator spun a bright fiery ball of red, he asked where it should go, and the boy answered, "In the eyes . . ."

"WHERE'S YOUR SNEAKER, DILLON?" asked his mother. It was the first thing she wanted to know. She was sitting on the lawn husking corn. She smiled but she looked worried.

"I forgot it," said Dillon.

"Forgot it?" said his mother. "Where?"

Dillon tried again. "I lost it."

"You lost your sneaker?" said his mother. She

was no longer smiling. "How on earth did you do that?"

When Dillon opened his mouth to speak he felt the nip of the loon. Right there in the soft part of his hand. Just as if he'd been nibbled again.

Dillon rubbed his hand. There was nothing there, but it still tickled. Dillon looked down at his bare foot.

"Can we change the subject?" he asked.

"If you insist," said his mother. "But I'd still like to know what happened to your sneaker."

Dillon sat down on the lawn, picked up an ear of corn, and began husking. He looked back at the island.

"What if a loon spoke to you?" he asked.

"To the best of my knowledge, loons can't speak to people," said Dillon's mother.

"But just say they could?" said Dillon. "What would it mean?"

"I don't really know," said his mother. She got up and went into the house. Her high-tops were under a lawn chair. Without thinking, Dillon reached for the left one. He slipped it onto his bare foot. It was deep and dark. But it was soft and supple too. Suddenly a rush of canvas and

rubber engulfed Dillon. Then a feeling of coolness. It was like the feeling of his mother's hand
on the back of his neck when she told him
about his name. She had not wanted to tell him.
She had not wanted to change reality. Dillon bit
his lip. His hand had begun to ache, right where
the loon had nipped it. Dillon took off his
mother's sneaker. He did not put it back under
the chair but placed it on the picnic bench beside his head.

Dillon's mother returned. She was carrying
his boat shoes.

"Put these on," she said. She looked down at
Dillon's feet. "And maybe you'll remember what
happened to your other sneaker."

"A bird borrowed it," said Dillon. He hoped
his mother wouldn't ask more. This time she
didn't.

Dillon put on his boat shoes and got to his
feet.

"Where are you going now?" asked his
mother.

"I've got some reading to do," said Dillon.

"I see," said his mother, returning to the corn
and wondering what her sneaker was doing on
the picnic bench.

Dillon went to the bookshelf on the porch. He bent his head sideways and scanned the titles. There was a row of dog-eared novels followed by books on fishing, boating, and cooking. On the bottom shelf was a series of field guides, most of them about birds. Dillon pulled out a slim volume tucked among them. It was a book about loons. On the inside cover *McDermott* was written in large blue letters. It had belonged to them.

Dillon turned the book over in his hands. Then he tucked it under his arm and carried it out to the front lawn. Daisy was plopped on the canvas swing.

"This swing smells like sunshine," she said.

"Sunshine doesn't smell," said Didier, who was passing by. He didn't bother to look at Daisy.

"Yes it does, doesn't it, Dillon?" said Daisy.

Dillon thought for a moment. "It smells yellow," he said.

"Yellow doesn't smell either," said Didier knowingly.

"Yellow does smell," Dillon insisted. He had never really noticed it before. But now he did. Sunshine smelled, and yellow too.

Didier rolled his eyes. "If you say so, Dillon."

"I do," said Dillon. He flattened himself on the lawn and looked skyward at the clouds which now looked like strands of cotton candy floating freely.

Dillon turned to his book and flipped through the pages. He began to read: "As the northern lakes begin to sparkle under a spring thaw, the loons arrive, drop down, and land in their summer homes . . . Loon calls echo across a moonlit lake with the eerie magic of a supernatural being . . . Loons swim, fly, they lay their heads over their backs and doze, but mostly they pursue, capture, and eat fish, and care for their feathers . . . Good places to nest and bring up their young are important considerations when choosing a territory . . ." Dillon stopped. His mother was calling him for lunch. Dillon closed the book. Tonight he would put it under his pillow. He hoped his head was porous, whatever that meant, and that he would wake up knowing.

That night Dillon fell asleep with the book over his face. He dreamed of loons. "Care of their feathers occupies loons throughout the day . . .

Loons lower their heads into the water and look around, in a gesture called peering. Loons disappear when they dive. Where do they go? What are they doing?" In the middle of it all was Dillon's sneaker.

12

*Once an old loon named Stonefeather defied his peers
and sang. He was answered by a wolf. And their
mournful serenade swelled into a joyous rhapsody.
From then on, there was no language among beasts
that could not be fathomed by all . . .*

DILLON WOKE UP with loon thoughts fresh in
his head. "I think my head is porous too," he
said to Didier.

Didier was busy cleaning his crayfish pots. He
stopped what he was doing and gave Dillon five.
"Way to go," he said. Then he handed Dillon a
slab of cold bacon. "Hold this, will you?" he
asked.

"What is it?" asked Dillon.

"It's bait for catching crayfish," explained Didier.

"What if they don't like it?" asked Dillon.

"They will," said Didier.

"But what if they don't," Dillon insisted.

Didier sighed and shook his head. "In life, Dillon, some things are and some things aren't. Grass is green. A flower does not grow into a tree. Crayfish like bacon." Didier kept reeling off examples.

"And a bird is not a person," Dillon interrupted him.

"Right," said Didier. "You got it."

Dillon nodded. But he was not sure he did get it. He was not certain that a loon was not in some way human. Or that a person was not in some way birdlike. Come to think of it, he was not sure of much. What if Didier was wrong? This was the first time that thought had occurred to Dillon.

Didier loaded the pots into his boat. He yanked the starter cord of the small outboard and putted off into the lake. Dillon went back to the house. His mother was painting. "I think my head's porous," he said.

Dillon's mother did not look up from her work. "We all have porous heads," she said.

"We do?" said Dillon. He felt surprised. And disappointed. He studied his mother's canvas. He thought he saw one thing, but even as he looked, it changed.

"What is it?" he asked.

"People," said his mother. Dillon followed the brushstrokes, the colorful curves and bends of paint, but no matter how he tried he could not make out that they were people.

Dillon shifted his weight from one foot to the other. He turned back toward the porch. A strange melting was happening inside him. He felt as though he might cry. He didn't know why. He wasn't hurt. He wasn't angry. Perhaps an old wound had opened. Maybe this was what happened when a head became porous.

Dillon's mother got up. She reached her arms around Dillon and held him tight. "You're going to be all right, Dillon," she said. "It takes time. It's okay to be mad. Okay to cry. This is part of who you are, Dillon. Try to accept it." Dillon's mother tugged his ear. "When you really get to know this Dillon Dillon, you will grow to love him just as we do."

Dillon nodded.

"Your mom was a scientist," said his mother. "We have a lot of her things packed away. She had a beautiful shell collection. When you're ready they're yours."

Dillon focused on the painting again. The shapes swelled and retreated. At last Dillon thought he could make out the figures. He was still not sure what was there on the canvas, but in his own mind he saw clearly the image of a bird and a boy.

As Dillon neared the island that day in his own boat, he let out a sharp birdlike cry. The loon cried back. It swam out to greet Dillon.

"You knew I would come," said Dillon, mooring the rowboat. The loon waddled up onto land. It raised one foot in the air and held it there. Then it shook the foot and placed it under its wing.

Dillon crouched down next to the loon. "My head is porous," he said. "What do you think of that?"

The loon squawked and waggled its foot again. Without thinking, Dillon stood and did the same thing. He lifted his foot in the air and shook hard. Anyone who saw him would have thought he was crazy. But in those moments Dillon felt anything but crazy.

"My sneaker?" Dillon asked after he'd put his foot down. He followed the loon to the spot where he'd left it. It was still there, embedded in the same mound of debris. But there was something in it.

"Is that an egg in my sneaker?" asked Dillon. It was an egg. A loon egg, deep olive brown with black spots. Dillon could feel its warmth without even touching it. Life was growing there in his sneaker. Dillon tried to move closer. But he was met with a flurry of wings and hoots. A second loon hurried past and flopped over to the sneaker. Then it squatted on the egg.

"Who are you?" asked Dillon. "Is that your egg?" Dillon turned to the first loon, who was paddling in the water. "I guess it belongs to both of you," he said. "And to me," he added. "After all, that's my sneaker that you've turned into a nest."

Dillon sat back on his heels. He watched the loons preen their feathers and stretch their wings. He looked down at his arms and legs and found himself longing for wings of his own that could carry him past the clouds. Longing for black-and-white patterned feathers etched in his skin. Longing for the knowing that he saw when he looked into the loon's red eye.

Dillon turned toward the water. The loon had paused and was waiting for him. Dillon knelt on a flat rock on the edge of the island. He saw a flash of the loon's white belly as it rolled over onto its side. Then the loon dove deeper. It was gone for a long time. When it came up, it held a fish crosswise in its beak. The loon scrambled back onto land and offered the fish to its mate sitting on the egg. Then it dove in again and came up with another fish. This time it offered its catch to Dillon.

"No, thank you," said Dillon. "I've already had breakfast." Dillon was confused. He didn't get it. Loons did not communicate with people. Dillon had read that. But these two were communicating with him. Did they think he was a bird? Was he a bird? Dillon threw the question to the wind rustling overhead and hoped for an answer.

Dillon didn't want to leave the island that day. As the sun dropped, bloated by the weight of day, and the shadows lengthened, Dillon began to feel that anything was possible. He watched the loons slide off the egg and climb back on, swapping places. And he began to feel their knowing, their simple faith in the order of the universe, in the way their feathers fell into a pattern. He wondered, if he were to stay on the island forever, would he grow feathers? Would his feet become weblike?

13

It is said that if a loon gives its flight call during a burial, the soul is being accompanied on its magical journey to the spirit world.

"HOW MANY TIMES have we told you not to put anything but paper down the toilet," said Dillon's mother. These were the words that greeted Dillon upon arriving home.

"Are you talking to me?" asked Dillon.

"I'm speaking to Daisy," said his mother.

Dillon followed her into the bathroom. Dillon's father was leaning over the toilet with a plunger, and Didier was rummaging through a toolbox.

"What's everyone doing in here?" asked Dillon.

"Daisy flushed Silly Putty down the toilet," explained Didier.

"It was a dragon," said Daisy. "And it fell into the enchanted lake."

Dillon's father coughed loudly. For a moment Dillon thought he might choke.

"It was Silly Putty," said Didier, handing his father a metal snake. "And it fell into the toilet."

"Daisy," said Dillon's father, "we're on a real lake. What's more enchanting than that? You don't have to use the toilet for make-believe."

"Do you know where your enchanted lake ends?" asked Didier. "A septic tank."

Daisy started to cry.

"Come on, now," said Dillon's mother. "Let's not crush her fantasy."

"I think we'd better," said Dillon's father. "Just a little." He straightened himself and dropped the plunger. "I can't do anything with this. We'll have to call the plumber."

"In the meantime we'll just have to use the outhouse," said Dillon's mother.

"What's an outhouse?" asked Daisy.

"A hole in the ground," said Didier.

"I want my dragon," whined Daisy.

"Dragons don't exist," said Didier.

"Yes they do," said Daisy. "Don't they, Dillon?"

Dillon didn't answer. He was thinking about the outhouse, back by the blueberry field. He had forgotten there was one. His grandparents had used it before there was plumbing. Because once there was no plumbing. Dillon's mind began to wander. Once there was no television. He looked down at his feet. Once he'd had both of his sneakers. Once he'd had different parents. But things had changed. Things were always changing. That was life.

Dillon went to bed that night hoping he wouldn't have to use the outhouse. Hoping he wouldn't have to rise in the dead of night and go outside. Didier had fallen asleep early. He had pulled the covers over his head to shut out the noises of night.

Dillon liked the nighttime noises: the dull croak of the bullfrogs, the gentle shivering of the poplars, the lapping of the waves against the shore. He had come to depend on these sounds, like an evening prayer or a bedtime lullaby, to send him to sleep.

Dillon woke up at three. He had to use the outhouse. He lay awake a long time wondering whether he could fall back to sleep. Whether he could wait until morning. Finally he got up. He took the flashlight his mother had left by the door and started across the lawn. The crickets were chirping. A bird was awake. Dillon was reminded of another of his teacher's favorite expressions: "The early bird gets the worm."

Dillon squinted, trying to make out shapes. It was funny how different things looked when they were masked in shadow. How different things felt and smelled. Dillon took a deep breath. Night had a scent. Darkness did too, just like sunshine and the color yellow.

Dillon paused before the outhouse. It was a sleepy little building with weeds sprouting from its seams and hinges. Dillon opened the door. It squeaked loudly. Dillon hoped there were no snakes or spiders. He stepped up to the wooden platform with a hole cut out of it and closed his eyes. A long time passed before anything hit the bottom. It echoed noisily, and Dillon felt a shiver crawl up his spine. He closed the door and hurried back across the grass. A white fairy-like form floated toward him. For a moment, Dillon thought it might be a ghost. He froze on the spot and waited as the shape came nearer. At last he could make out Daisy's nightgown.

"Daisy," Dillon whispered.

"Will you wait for me?" she asked.

"Hurry," said Dillon.

"Daddy says you're my uncle," called Daisy from behind the wooden door.

"Your cousin," Dillon corrected her.

"But I want you to be my uncle," said Daisy. "And my cousin. And my brother," she added.

Dillon couldn't help smiling. "All right," he said.

"Didier said dragons don't exist," said Daisy.

"Hmmm," said Dillon. He was not sure what he was supposed to say. He had believed in Santa Claus and the Easter Bunny and the Tooth Fairy until he was eight. And even after he found out the truth he continued to hope that it wasn't true.

"They do exist," said Dillon finally. Then he added, "Somewhere."

When Daisy was finished, Dillon took her hand and led her back toward the house.

"Wait," cried Daisy.

"What for?" asked Dillon impatiently.

"Spencer," said Daisy.

Dillon had forgotten about Daisy's imaginary friend. "I didn't know Spencer was with you," he said flatly.

"He is," said Daisy. "And he's afraid of the dark."

Dillon nodded. A bullfrog ribbited in the bushes.

"I'll bet it's a dragon," said Daisy knowingly.

"Could be," said Dillon, who was still thinking about Spencer.

14

Once a small girl was taught a song by the loons. Years later, when she sang that song, she was transformed into a loon. It is she who guides the Indians back to the shore when they are lost in the fog . . .

DILLON STOOD IN THE MIDDLE of a kingdom, beside a sand castle he had constructed with Daisy. "Eunice," he shouted. He hoped she would answer. He hoped her voice would echo back from some far corner of the lake.

"Eunice," he cried again. And he felt that he was freeing himself from some mysterious spell.

"Who's Eunice?" asked Daisy, who was dropping clamshells in the castle's moat.

Dillon shrugged. "An imaginary friend," he said, pushing his boat into the water. "Like Spencer."

"Is Eunice going with you?" Daisy wanted to know.

"Yes," said Dillon. Eunice was always with him. Sort of. At least the memory of Eunice standing in line at the gas station. The possibility that she was as nice as she looked. And the hope that they might meet again. "She's coming," said Dillon as he slipped slowly away from the shore and rowed toward the island just as he'd done every day for nearly two weeks.

"This is Eunice," Dillon announced to the loons. "She's a friend." Dillon could hardly believe what he was doing. Not only was he talking to birds but he was speaking with invisible people. One of the loons was swimming close to the island's edge. It did a foot waggle. The other sat quietly on the egg in Dillon's sneaker. Dillon guessed she was the female. She was not interested in Eunice. The male loon dove in, brought up a fish, and offered it to Dillon.

"They think I'm a bird," Dillon said to Eunice. "Maybe I am a bird," he continued. "What do you think?" Dillon knelt down and stared into the blueness in front of him. He looked at his arms and legs, his body. He was sorry Eunice was not really there to answer him.

The loon who had offered Dillon a fish sidled up close to him. He nipped at the boomerang at Dillon's waist.

Dillon got to his feet. He pulled the wooden arc from his belt and held it in the air. It had been a while since he had thrown it. "This is a boomerang," he said. "It's an Australian throwing club." Now he sounded like Didier. "I'm not very good at it, but it's supposed to come back when you throw it."

Dillon tossed the boomerang out toward the trees. It seemed to stop in midair. Then, with a downward tilt, it turned and flew back. This time it landed at Dillon's feet. Dillon's father had said that was its destiny. To always come back. Did we all have a destiny? Dillon wondered at this very big idea growing in his head. Was it his destiny to be on this island? To be a bird, if only for a short time? Because he was a bird in some small way. He had to be. His porous head had not gotten it wrong.

The loon who had been sitting on the egg got to its feet. It shuffled around its nest. Dillon mimicked the movements. He did not have feathers to preen. But he rubbed his arms and legs and felt the hairs stiffen and fall back against his skin.

Dillon watched the loons swap places on the egg. One would shuffle down to the water for something to eat and the other would sit peacefully on the egg, eyes closed. Dillon did not forget that he had brought an imaginary friend that day. Every so often he would turn to Eunice. "Would you like a bite of my sandwich?" he asked. Eunice said yes. She loved ham sandwiches just as Dillon did. "Do I look like a bird to you?" he asked again. But Eunice would not answer that question.

Dillon rowed home, a current of unexplained joy flowing through his body. He began to sing. "Row, row, row your boat," he crooned. He turned to where Eunice would be sitting were she there. "Will you join me?" he asked. Eunice gave an imaginary nod. And as Dillon rowed the final stretch home, he could almost hear her voice blend with his, bounce off the waves, and disappear behind the distant hills.

Later that day Didier brought home his first real catch. He had spent hours trolling, a solitary seafarer with his flute, and had not caught a thing. Dillon admired his perseverance, his patience. Dillon would have given up after the first day. Now Didier appeared like an apparition before them all, four trout hanging from a string.

His father slapped him on the back. "Congratulations," he said.

"Way to go," said Dillon.

"Are we going to eat them?" cried Daisy, making a face.

"You bet we are," answered Didier. Dillon's stomach turned. The fish looked still alive, suspended in midair, their eyes wide open.

"Who's going to clean them?" asked Dillon's mother. "Any volunteers?"

"I'll clean them," said Didier. He spread newspaper on the ground and pulled out his army knife. Dillon watched as he slit open the trout and carved through the layers. Didier kicked off his sneakers and tossed them onto the deck of the boathouse. Dillon eyed them for a long time. Then he walked over to them. They were worn white canvas. Didier had scribbled something in black ink along the rubber soles. Dillon was barefoot. He slipped into the left sneaker. It was big, but he could feel the sweat clinging to its sides. He could feel the blood flowing. These shoes were alive. Dillon put on the other one and walked in a circle.

"Hey," cried Didier, holding something in the air. "Look what I found."

"It looks like a tiddlywink," said his father. It was a tiddlywink, sea green. Just like the one Dillon had given to Eunice. Maybe it was the one Dillon had given to Eunice. Dillon hoped so. He liked the idea of its finding its way back to him. But of course that would mean that Eunice had lost it.

"Can I have it?" Dillon asked.

"Be my guest," said Didier. He tossed the tiddlywink to Dillon and returned to his work.

"Could a tiddlywink find its way back to me?" Dillon asked. "Like a boomerang?"

"That's an interesting question," said Dillon's

father. He closed his eyes and thought about it.

"Let's say I'd given it to someone," said Dillon. "Someone not far away."

Dillon's father opened his eyes. "Given the number of tiddlywinks in circulation, given their size, given how often things get lost, given the law of probability, it's unlikely. But it could happen," he added.

Dillon dropped the sea-green tiddlywink into his pocket. It was true that the tiddlywink makers produced millions of tiddlywinks. It could belong to anyone. But somehow Dillon knew that this was the tiddlywink he had given to Eunice at the gas station. Eunice must have lost it, and it had found its way back to him. Dillon slid his hand into his pocket and felt for the tiddlywink. If he closed his eyes and squeezed it hard enough, he could almost feel Eunice's fingerprints, see her wavy hair, her bright smile.

Supper was a feast. Grilled fish, baked potatoes, blueberries, and lemonade, tart and cool. Dillon's mother took pictures of them seated around the picnic table with its wobbly legs and chipped paint.

"Say cheese, everyone," she called. The lens caught perfectly the splash of summertime color. But at the same time Dillon realized that a picture captured so little of what they felt. It was the same with the photo of his first parents. He could see their smiles, but he could never really know what they were feeling, not deep inside anyway.

15

Throughout time, loons have been revered as weather forecasters. And the long lonely wail of the loon means a storm is on the way . . .

THE NERVOUS FLITTER OF LEAVES on the poplars, the mischievous rattling of the bullfrogs in the reeds, the absence of the crickets' song all announced to Dillon that a storm was coming. He could feel anticipation building inside himself.

"It looks like it's going to be a beauty," said Dillon's father. "Let's get the boats in."

Dillon helped Didier haul the boats up on the lawn and flip them upside down. They took in the hammock and the chairs, the swing that smelled like sunshine. When they closed the windows and shut the blinds, it seemed as if the whole cottage had folded in upon itself.

Dillon watched the sky bubbling like a cauldron, the dark clouds overflowing like froth. The loons would know how to shelter themselves, their egg. But Dillon still found himself hoping that they would be spared the brunt of the storm.

They had an early supper before the winds started, bread and corn chowder. Dillon opened the card table and set up the Scrabble game.

"Anyone want to play?" he asked.

"I'll play," said Didier. He took a seat across from Dillon. Didier spelled I-C-E. Dillon placed an N in front of I-C-E.

"N-I-C-E," he said out loud.

"Six points," said Didier.

"N-I-C-E," Dillon repeated. Again he thought of Eunice Schroeder. He wondered what she was doing at this very minute. Was she still on the lake? Was she playing Scrabble somewhere? Would she too be caught up in the storm, quivering as the thunder and the lightning burst forth from the heavens?

"Tell me a story," Daisy demanded, curling herself up in a chair.

"I'll read you a book," said her mother. Daisy opened *Blueberries for Sal*. As the wind roared and sang and beat against the house, Dillon listened to the kuplink, kuplank, kuplunk of Sal dropping berries into her bucket. Every now and then the lights flicked on and off. Finally the power went out and they were left in darkness. Dillon's mother was prepared, though, with flashlights and candles.

"What if it never stopped raining?" Dillon asked. It was a fear he'd always had but never voiced.

"That's stupid," said Didier. "And impossible."

"Just what if?" insisted Dillon.

"Easy," said Didier. "We'd all drown. Does that make you feel better?" Daisy started to cry.

"Could you find something else to talk about?" said Dillon's mother.

Dillon went back to Scrabble. He spelled S-W-A-L-L-O-W. Didier added I-N-G.

"I won," he said. Dillon shrugged. He scooped up the letters and poured them into the box. Then he sat back in his chair and watched the shadows pass over their faces. He did not know when he fell asleep, nor was he aware of being lifted or of his father's heavy gait as he carried Dillon up to the loft and tucked him into bed. But as Dillon slept he heard, "I love you, Dillon Dillon," over and over in his head. He did not know if it was a message carried by the wind or the gentle voice of his father blessing his sleep.

Dillon woke to the rhythmic lapping of the rain, steady enough so that he knew it would last for days. He played jacks with Daisy and chess with his father. When he beat Didier at arm wrestling, he wondered if the rain had turned the world inside out.

"Way to go, Dill," Didier congratulated him.

"Can I go to the island?" asked Dillon. It was the third time he had asked that day.

"No," said his mother firmly. Dillon did not ask again.

As dusk fell, Dillon heard the call of a loon, clear and crisp. He could not help but call back.

"Dillon," said his mother, annoyed. Dillon pressed his face against the window. He thought he could just make out the shape of a bird swimming close to shore.

After three days the rain stopped. Dillon felt the triumph of the sun as it broke through the clouds. The smells of the earth, pine, moss, lichen rose from the damp spongy ground. It was the scent of new life. Dillon breathed it in heartily. He flipped his boat over and hauled it down to the shore.

Dillon began to row. The water level had risen and the water was colder. Dillon could feel the coolness settle around his ankles and wrists. It had nestled deep into the handles of the oars and it would take days of warm sunshine to pull it out.

The island did not loom as before. Rather, it seemed to have sunk deeper into the lake. The storm had snapped branches from the trees, pulled moss and lichen away from the bedrock. Dillon's heartbeat quickened as he tripped over fragments of driftwood and broken shells. He didn't let out his breath until he reached his sneaker. It was soggy and wet and wore a double crown of cattails, moss, and twigs. But the egg had survived. It was still there, and the two loons were swapping turns sitting on it.

"Hi," said Dillon. "It's me. Are you guys all right?"

The loon closer to Dillon hooted. Then it wobbled over to Dillon and pecked him on the hand. Dillon was used to this by now.

"I was worried about you," said Dillon.

The second loon's eyes popped open and it began preening its feathers. The first loon pecked Dillon's hand again. It pecked again and again until Dillon followed it back to the water's edge.

"What do you want?" Dillon asked. He knew the answer. The loon wanted Dillon to dive under. To go deep down within the folds of the water.

Dillon shook his head. "It's cold down there," he said. But the loon did not give up. It pecked Dillon's ankle. Then it looked at Dillon, its red eye shining, and it seemed to speak. "Don't be afraid. I will take you. I will show you. I will be by your side."

"No," said Dillon again. He didn't want to go under the water. He didn't want to feel the cold envelop his body. But the loon would not take its eyes off him. And at last Dillon had to go.

Dillon pulled off his T-shirt, his socks, and his shoes. He unstrapped his watch and spread his things across a flat rock.

The loon slipped into the water. It lowered its head and looked around. Dillon had often wondered where the loon went when it dove under. Now he would find out.

Dillon balanced on a ledge, arms spread wide. Then he closed his eyes and let himself fall. When he opened his eyes he was immersed in a whole new world. Plants sprouted from the pale sandy lake bed and wavered back and forth. Minnows darted fearlessly in and around his flailing arms and legs. Dillon felt the cold embrace him as he followed the loon deeper. But then he hit a sunny spot and warmth swelled around him.

The loon surfaced first and waited for Dillon. Dillon popped his head out of the water. "I did it," he said. Then he dove under again and again. He floated and turned in the gentle currents. He skimmed the bottom, turning back plants and rocks as though he were searching for something. Maybe he was. His parents. Some clue to the great mystery of life.

Could a boy become a bird? Dillon stood on the ledge and asked himself that question. He asked himself a dozen times each day. He did not know the answer, but he felt himself changing. When he looked at Didier, he no longer saw a shadow much bigger than his own. He saw another boy struggling with his own problems. When he looked at Daisy, he saw a little girl caught between reality and imagination. And he remembered what it was like at five to be unsure of each. When he looked at his parents, he saw two adults whose gestures often puzzled him. But, more than that, he saw two people who loved him. Dillon began to understand why his mother smiled when she scolded him. Why his father laughed when he was nervous. Other things he did not understand and probably never would. But maybe that was life.

16

Once upon a time a loon met a blind boy. The boy
followed the loon to a lake, and there, minding the
loon's example, he dove three times and so regained
his sight . . .

DILLON HAD NEVER SLEPT away from home.
Nonetheless, he rolled up his sleeping bag and
prepared his knapsack as though he'd done it
countless times. He packed extra clothes, a
flashlight, batteries, food, his boomerang and
watch. Only then did he ask his mother.

"Can I sleep on the island?" he said.

His mother paused. Dillon knew that she was

making a mental list of all the things that could happen to him alone on an island.

"I don't know if that's a good idea," she said.

"Nothing's going to happen," said Dillon hopefully. His mother raised her eyebrows. She turned to Dillon's father.

"What about asking Didier to go along?" his father suggested.

"No," said Dillon. "I want to do it alone."

"All right," said his father.

Dillon left after supper. He pushed his boat into the water and climbed in. Daisy handed him a firefly in a jar. "It'll be like a night-light," she said.

"Thanks," said Dillon. Rowing was easy. It was the time of day when the water was calm. The sun had just begun to slip from the sky. Every now and then a fish would jump out of the lake and spin in a wide arc, startling Dillon.

Dillon pulled the boat up to his usual spot and stepped onto the island. He wandered over to the nest. One of the loons was sitting on the egg. As Dillon approached, it flapped its wings and let out a hoot.

"It's just me," whispered Dillon. "I've come to stay with you tonight." The other loon, who had been swimming nearby, climbed onto the ledge. It ruffled its feathers and came toward Dillon. Dillon bent his elbows and flapped his arms a couple of times. Then he let out a hoot. By now Dillon could almost cry just like one of them. And when he called out, he was always answered.

The loon approached its mate sitting on the egg and nudged her. She slipped off the egg. Dillon moved closer. Both loons watched him, trusting, until at last he mustered the courage to touch the egg. He stroked it lightly.

"I am a bird," he whispered, and he believed it. The trees believed too. And the waves and the wind. Dillon stood back. The loon reclaimed its place on the egg. It let out a cry. Dillon answered, his voice crossing the lake and echoing back. Then all distinction melted away. Feathers, arms, skin, beaks, noses. They were all simply alive, breathing.

Dillon sat cross-legged. The last streaks of daylight were disappearing from the sky and dusk was falling like a fine powder. Dillon watched the darkness soak into the scenery surrounding him, the first stars begin to twinkle, and he was suddenly aware that the island had an evening of its own. The pale blue patches of lichen, the puddles of white sand sprinkled among the pines all glistened in a wash of gently falling shade. Dillon listened to the sounds around him muffled by the water. He checked his watch. July 14, 9:07.

Dillon unrolled his sleeping bag and spread it on a carpet of soft moss and lichen not far from the egg. The stars were brilliant, the moon was a half-disc. Dillon set the jar with the firefly beside his head. He slept more deeply than he ever had. His dreams were all of magic and hope. At dawn he woke briefly, roused by the first rays of the sun. Then he fell back asleep. Somewhere in between dreams and wakefulness, he saw a loon with a boy on its back circling the island. And he wondered, was that boy him?

17

Once, in gratitude for having his youth returned, a hunter threw a necklace of tiny polished stones to the loon. As they fell around its neck, stones became its beautiful plumage . . .

DILLON ROLLED OVER onto his back. Something brushed his cheek. He felt the brisk peck of a bird on his temple. Dillon opened his eyes.

"Good morning to you too," he said. The loon continued to peck Dillon until he pulled back the cover of his sleeping bag and stood up. Dillon followed the loon to the island's edge. He leaned down and splashed water on his face. The loon dove into the lake, flapped its wings, and splashed. Every so often it would nip the feathers on its belly. The loon dove under. Seconds later it brought up a fish.

Dillon reached for his knapsack. He bit into the peanut butter and jelly sandwich that he'd brought, along with a carton of juice. The loon dove under another time and brought up a second fish. Then he took his place on the egg while his mate bathed.

"When's it going to be my turn?" teased Dillon. He knew he would not get a turn, but it was fun to pretend. Dillon observed the egg. It had been there just over twenty days. A loon egg incubated in under a month. Dillon remembered this from his reading. Soon this egg would hatch. A baby loon would burst out of the shell. Dillon hoped he would be there.

Dillon sipped his juice. A group of laughing girls passed in a canoe. Dillon strained for a better look. He wondered if Eunice Schroeder was among them. He uttered her name, but there was no wind that day to carry it across the water. And it remained on the island like a tightly guarded secret.

The morning idled by. No one moved. Not the loons, not Dillon. Overhead, the leaves hung steady on their branches. One would have thought that time stood still. But Dillon knew better. The sun had been creeping steadily higher into the sky. And when Dillon could no longer see his shadow, he knew he should row home.

"It's about time," called his father. He was tending the barbecue. Hot dogs and hamburgers.

Dillon sat down on the picnic bench next to Daisy.

"You're sitting on Spencer," cried Daisy.

Dillon jumped up. "Sorry," he said.

"There's an empty place next to me," said Didier, scowling at Daisy. "At least, I think there is."

Dillon sat down next to his brother. He hoped no one would ask questions.

"How'd it go?" asked Didier.

Dillon sighed. "It went fine," he said.

Dillon's father set a plate of warmed buns on the table.

"Was it scary?" Daisy wanted to know.

"No," said Dillon. "It was peaceful. It was nice."

"Were there any dragons?" Daisy asked. Dillon was careful not to say no.

"I didn't see any," he said.

Dillon's mother brought a platter of french fries to the table. Dillon shoveled a heap onto his plate. He did not want to use his hands. Suddenly he bent over his plate, opened his mouth, and caught a fry. "Got one," he said.

"Dillon!" cried his mother. "That's not funny."

Dillon finished his lunch. He got up from the picnic table, but he could not seem to stop wiggling and fidgeting. He ran his hand along a wooden sawhorse. It was full of splinters. Dillon got one in the palm of his hand.

"Sit still and be brave," said his mother. She poked and probed with tweezers. Dillon bit his lip. Finally she pulled the splinter out. Dillon watched the blood bubble to the surface of his skin.

"Can I put the Band-Aid on it?" asked Daisy.

"It's up to Dillon," said his mother.

"Go ahead," said Dillon.

Daisy pulled open the backings of a Band-Aid and spread it carefully over the palm of Dillon's hand. "I'm going to be a veterinarian when I grow up," she said.

"You mean a doctor," said Dillon.

"No, I mean a veterinarian," insisted Daisy. "What are you going to be?"

"A bird," said Dillon, not sure if he was teasing or not.

Dillon did not return to the island that day. The palm of his hand hurt too much to row. Instead he picked blueberries with Daisy. At bedtime Didier put a book of fishing chants under his pillow.

"Will you know all the songs in the morning?" asked Dillon.

"Depends," said Didier.

"On what?" asked Dillon. "On how porous your head is?"

"Yes." Didier nodded absently.

Dillon rolled over. He wasn't tired. He couldn't sleep.

"Do you always play music when you troll?" he asked.

"No," answered Didier. "Sometimes I just wait. And I will the fish to come."

"Do they?" asked Dillon.

"Not always," said Didier.

Dillon thought about what his brother had said. And he wondered if the fish were like the boomerang. If they had a destiny. If their destiny was Didier or something else.

"Any more questions?" asked Didier.

Dillon was silent for a moment. Then he spoke. "Can a boy become a bird?" he asked.

"No," said Didier. "Only over thousands of years. Through evolution."

"I think I'm a bird sometimes," said Dillon.

"Maybe you were a bird," said Didier. "But now you're a boy."

"Now I'm a boy," repeated Dillon. And he drifted off to sleep repeating to himself, "Now I'm a boy."

18

Once a loon and a crow were fishermen who quarreled at sea. The crow knocked the loon on the head, cut out its tongue, and stole its catch. Now when the loon utters its humanlike cry it is the wronged fisherman trying to tell the sad story of this cruel treatment . . .

"DO YOU WANT to bait the crayfish pots with me?" Didier asked. Dillon had been waiting for this. He'd been hoping that one day Didier would ask him to join him. But now that he did, Dillon was no longer sure.

"No, thanks," he said.

"Suit yourself," said Didier. "You don't know what you're missing."

Dillon shrugged. "Maybe another day," he said. But in his mind he thought probably never. He had come to believe that the crayfish pots, the fishing flies belonged to Didier. They were his destiny. He, Dillon, had another destiny.

Dillon loaded his own boat and set off. Summer had ripened faultlessly. The berries were bursting on their vines and the wild roses and honeysuckle bounced gaily on their stems. The air was alive with crickets chirping and frogs ribbiting in happy unison.

Dillon neared the island. He secured his boat and went straight to his sneaker. To the loon egg. The female had climbed off the nest and was watching it. She looked at Dillon sharply.

"Hi there," said Dillon. "Where's your friend?" The second loon appeared. It did not look at Dillon but at the egg. All eyes were focused on the egg. The chick had begun pecking and had carved a full circle in the top of it. The egg was about to hatch. Dillon knelt down beside the two loons. He listened to the chick chirping as it worked. A long time passed before it flopped out. When it did, it fell clumsily into the nest. It was small and wet and covered with soft blackish down. Its belly was white.

"Welcome," Dillon whispered, filled with emotion. He looked at his watch. He could not remember his parents or his own birth, but something deep inside of him responded to the chick's arrival on this particular day and time. July 20, 11:01.

The chick did not leave the nest that day. It spent most of its time crawling under and over its parents. Occasionally it would nestle under the wing of its mother and then climb onto her back. When the chick peeped softly, its mother called back. Dillon did not know what they were saying. But he could imagine.

"Where am I?" the little bird might ask.

"Home," the mother would say.

The little bird would be hungry. "I want to eat."

The parent would comfort it. "Food is coming."

"Who is that?" the chick would ask as it noticed Dillon for the first time.

"That's Dillon Dillon," the mother would answer. "He's one of us."

"He's one of us," Dillon said out loud. But he did not approach the chick. He let it quietly and slowly grow accustomed to its surroundings, the damp ground, the crackle of twigs, the water washing against the shore, and the feel of its parents always close by. Dillon thought of his own parents, the parents he had now. And he realized that he too could feel their presence even when they weren't nearby.

Dillon stayed for the loon's first feeding. For its first nap. He reveled in the happy sight of the broken eggshell crumbled in his sneaker. As he rowed home that day, he felt privileged that the loons had sought him out. They had chosen his shoe. It could not be chance. It had to be destiny. Dillon looked at his watch one last time and stamped the date in his memory. He would later celebrate this day and remember it as the time of his own rebirth.

When Dillon returned the next day, the chick was in the water swimming alongside its parents. When it tried to climb onto the back of one parent, the other loon would appear and the baby would swim toward it. As it got closer, that parent would swim off and the other would appear. This continued until the baby loon was carried safely to a small cove at the end of the island. This would be the baby loon's nursery.

The baby was finished with its nest. Now it would need a shallow shelter, protected from strong winds and waves, until it could fend for itself.

Dillon observed the chick pecking the side of its mother's head for food. He listened to its short sharp cries as it waited for its meal. And he smiled as he watched the parent loon approach the baby with a fish held crosswise in its beak. Sometimes the chick would grasp it in its mouth and turn it skillfully. Other times the fish would flop back into the water and the parent would retrieve it.

Dillon rejoiced in these rituals, but something had changed. He had waited for the egg to hatch almost as eagerly as if it were his own. Now that the chick was born, he felt strangely left out. He was allowed to watch, but he got no more pecks. The loons still swam close to the island, but they rarely climbed onto land. Only once did one of them return to the nest. It pecked at some sticks and tore away a piece of lichen. Then it looked at Dillon with its red eye, and Dillon was taken back to that first day of summer and reminded of the grasshopper.

Dillon knelt down beside the lopsided nest.

He eyed a corner of his sneaker buried under the layers of debris. It had served its purpose.

"Do you mind if I take back my sneaker?" Dillon asked.

The loon laughed heartily. It did not seem to mind. Dillon reached under the nest and pulled out his sneaker. He held it in his hand. It was heavy with dirt and moisture. And it had lost its shape. Dillon could not resist putting it on. He kicked off his boat shoe and pushed his foot into the sneaker. It was soggy and felt nearly a size smaller, but Dillon kept it on. He wore it home that day. When he left the island, he let out a hoot. And when the loons responded with a glorious cry, Dillon felt he'd reclaimed some of his space.

Didier greeted Dillon with a slap on the shoulder. "You don't know what you've been missing," he said and he shoved a bucket in front of Dillon. Two big-clawed crayfish scrambled up the sides.

Dillon smiled. "Way to go," he said. In his heart he felt happy that the day had been a triumph for Didier too.

"By the way," said Didier. "You know you're wearing two different shoes?"

Dillon nodded. He climbed the stairs to the loft to search for the mate to his sneaker. It was stashed under his bed next to a pile of comics. Dillon pulled it out and put it on. He wandered from one spot to another, feeling weightless. He kept his sneakers on until right before bedtime. The fireflies had begun to glow when he finally took them off and lined them up by the door alongside Didier's moccasins, Daisy's sandals, his mother's high-tops, and his father's boat shoes.

19

THE WEEKS THAT FOLLOWED rolled into one another like gentle waves. Dillon still went to the island almost daily. He sat on a rocky ledge and let his mind travel back in time. Now and again he thought of Eunice. He had not lost hope that someday they might meet again. He thought of the loons, of his being a bird. Of the spell that seemed to have been broken when the chick tumbled out of the egg. Of destiny. Of his sneaker. Of all the what ifs. He would have liked to tell all of this to Eunice. The story of his family and of himself. He knew she would listen. And she would smile.

Dillon no longer expected the loons to greet

him. They were busy teaching the chick about life. They would leave it for brief periods but they would always return.

Then one day Dillon found the chick swimming alone among a crop of cattails.

"Hey, little guy," he said. "What are you doing?"

The chick began splashing and let out a high-pitched wail. It was the first time it had spoken to Dillon. Dillon moved down to the edge of the water. He reached his hand toward the baby loon. The chick swam up very close to him. For a moment, Dillon thought that it might peck him. But it let out another hoot.

"Where are your mother and father?" Dillon asked. Dillon knew they would be diving. He knew too that they would be back. A baby chick could not feed itself until it was at least eight weeks old.

The baby loon swam away from him. It bobbed its head in and out of the water several times, then returned. It began preening its feathers. But it stayed close to Dillon.

Dillon picked up a stick and began digging. He was very near the spot where his father had buried the silver dollars.

"There are three silver dollars somewhere around here," he said to the chick. "Do you want to help me look for them?" The chick nibbled its feathers. It was not listening.

Dillon poked and dug but unearthed nothing but worms and insects. From off in the distance the notes from Didier's flute reached him. The little chick cocked its head.

"That's Didier," said Dillon. "That's his flute you hear."

Dillon let out a low loon wail. He waited for an answer. None came. Dillon shifted his weight from one foot to the other. He had begun to feel uncomfortable. He looked at his watch. It was nearly eleven o'clock. The loons had to be back soon. So Dillon waited.

At noon he did a foot waggle.

At one he took a swim. At two Dillon began to worry. He rowed home for some lunch but was back on the island by three. By now the baby loon was yelping. It had tired of splashing about and had perched itself on a pile of flattened twigs and leaves. It was hungry. But it was not able to fish for itself.

Dillon reached into his knapsack. He found a corner of bread and two stale cookies. "Here," he said. "Have some of these." The loon swam over to him and pecked at the bread but it would not eat.

At last Dillon had to leave. Afternoon had mellowed into a deep golden hue. "Your parents will return soon," he whispered. "And I'll be back first thing in the morning," he added.

Dillon rowed home. He strained to hear the call of the loons, for some clue as to where they were. He searched the shore for the bold outline of their feathers. But the shoreline did not move. Phrases and reminders of all that he'd read exploded in Dillon's head. "In the early weeks of life loon parents and their chicks are together most of the time . . . Loon chicks are dependent on their parents for feeding and protection for at least two months . . . Loons do not leave their young before three months, when the family breaks up . . ." A cold sweat broke out on Dillon's skin. Perhaps the loons had been hiding. Maybe they had been testing the baby chick. Dillon hoped so.

The next day the parent loons had not returned. Nor did they return the day after. Dillon spent as much time as he could on the island. But the baby stayed close to the cove and would not come near him. At times it would flap its wings furiously. At other times it would sit motionless, rocked by the waves.

"Don't worry," Dillon would whisper. "Your parents will be back." And in his heart he kept hoping they would. He caught small sunfish and left them on the ledge, but he never knew if they were eaten by the chick or a predator. He himself had lost his appetite.

"Have some mud pie," said Daisy when he returned home. She offered Dillon a slice topped with teaberries and baby pinecones. "It's Spencer's birthday."

"I'm not hungry," said Dillon. But Daisy insisted.

"Just take a little taste," she said. Dillon closed his eyes and pretended to eat. Cakes were for celebrating. But a knot had begun to form in the pit of his stomach. Deep inside, he knew there was nothing to celebrate.

20

EVERYONE MAKES MISTAKES. Mr. Joe Sargeant made a mistake when he shot at the pair of birds he saw flying low across the sky. He thought they were ducks, but they were loons.

"Holy Toledo," he murmured as he stood over the two birds. He looked around to see if he'd been noticed. He did not want to be caught. Loons were a protected species. He would have to pay a hefty fine, and his hunting license might be revoked.

Mr. Sargeant shrugged to himself, forgetting that even if they had been ducks, he was still breaking the law. He shouldn't have been hunting on the lake. Hunting season did not begin until October. It was written and posted everywhere.

He pulled up a bunch of reeds and tossed them over the bodies. Then he wiped out his footprints in the mud and left.

The loons lay cradled by the waves until the current washed them under and carried them farther into the lake. They floated and turned with the random movements of the water until at last they were swept into a crayfish pot, which happened to belong to Didier.

Didier was not prepared for what he found. He had risen that morning and baited his crayfish pots as he did every day. He'd motored out into the lake with his small outboard and dropped them. Then he'd headed to a secluded cove, where he'd spent the morning trolling. He had returned home for lunch. He'd eaten a grilled cheese sandwich with onions, a handful of pretzels, and a bowl of blueberries swamped with milk. Then he'd played two rounds of Go Fish with Daisy. He'd puttered around in the boathouse for most of the afternoon. And he'd actually thought of waiting a day to check his pots so that he could paint the stern of his boat. All of these details he recalled later. When he finally did haul in his pots, one was heavier than it ought to be. He had weighted them. And sometimes a cluster of reeds or even garbage found its way into the pots. But when Didier checked the net, he did not expect to find the bodies of two dead loons.

Their feathers were wet but perfectly aligned in a beautiful pattern of inkwash. Their red eyes gazed into nothingness. Didier coughed nervously. He felt a bubble rise from the pit of his stomach. He was suddenly aware of the pinkish cast of the sky that stained everything around him and a smell that was not just of day's end.

Didier settled the pots on the bottom of the boat. He sat very still for a while and willed himself to listen, to quietly decipher the sounds that surrounded him. The bullfrogs rumbling, the trees rustling, the far-off sound of a baby loon crying mournfully. For Didier these sounds would always remain a sad song of loss.

Didier revved the motor of his small outboard and headed homeward. Dillon spotted him from a distance. He watched Didier ease up on the motor and turn at a certain point toward shore. He wondered as always if Didier had caught anything.

"I found them in my crayfish pots," said Didier matter-of-factly. "They were at the bottom of the lake."

Dillon bent forward for a closer look. A lump rose in his throat. He wanted to scream or shout. But he stood silent, feeling the tears well in the corners of his eyes.

Didier lowered his head. He did not hear his father approach.

"What have you got?" his father asked. But his father was no more prepared than the others. "Damn poachers," he said. He rested his hands on Dillon's neck and began to rub his shoulders.

A deep sadness washed over Dillon. A sadness mixed with a strange wonder at the beauty of life and the grimness of death. Finally he managed to speak. "I knew them," he said. "I knew them well."

"That's life," said Didier, summing it up and shaking his head.

Dillon guessed Didier was right. Life ended

with death. It did not matter that no one knew when or why.

It was well after seven o'clock when Mr. O'Leary came out of his house that day. He strolled down to the shore in his T-shirt and swim trunks. He lifted his hand to his forehead and scanned the horizon. But he did not dive into the lake that day. For the first time that anyone could remember, Mr. O'Leary did not take his late-afternoon swim.

"No," Dillon reminded himself as he crossed the lawn for the umpteenth time. "Nothing in life is certain."

"Do you think we ought to bury them?" Didier asked. He'd emptied the pots, and the bodies were lying on a patch of grass.

"It's up to you boys," said his dad. "But if you're going to bury them, you ought to do it soon."

Dillon got the shovel and hoe from the boathouse. Didier wrapped the bodies in a simple net. They took the net between them and wandered back past the outhouse, across the field. In his head Dillon heard the kuplink, kuplank, kuplunk of blueberries striking the sides of a tin pail. They neared the stone wall that marked their property. And in a small, isolated glade, surrounded by brown-eyed Susans and Queen Anne's lace, they began to dig. Dillon overturned earth, thinking of how just the other day he'd been digging for the three silver coins. When they'd dug deeply enough, Didier dropped the net into the hole and they laid the loons to rest. As Dillon heaped the final shovel of earth over the grave, he was reminded of how parallel lives could be. How like his own life was that of the chick. And he was conscious of all the loons had given to him. They had given him eyes, feet, and feathers to fly. They had given him a voice. He was a boy, but in some small way he'd been a bird too.

Sweat stood out on Dillon's wrists and temples. The boomerang cut into his waist. It made him think of what his father had said. Of destiny. It was hard to believe that this could be the loons' destiny. Even harder to accept. Dillon could not stop wondering where they would go. He could not help hoping that they might meet again.

Dillon put down the shovel. He did a foot waggle because it just seemed right. Didier had brought along his flute. He lifted it to his lips and played a fishing chant. The notes turned and twisted on the breeze and finally died out like wisps of wind.

As evening finally fell, Didier and Dillon walked back across the blueberry field, past the outhouse, toward home, their shadows melting into one.

Dillon's father was roasting marshmallows with Daisy and Spencer. Dillon and Didier halfheart-edly joined in. Their father piled kindling onto the fire and watched it take hold. Then they speared the marshmallows with sticks and watched the outer shells bubble and char.

Dillon caught his father looking at him.

"Penny for your thoughts," said Dillon.

His father hesitated. Then he spoke. "I was thinking of your mother, Dillon. My sister, Maggie." He tripped over each word. "She was a biologist. I guess we've told you that. She liked to come here, to watch the loons. She used to talk about them as though they were people. She used to talk to them. Sometimes I thought she was one of them." Dillon's father nodded his head. He went on. "I was thinking of that today,

Dillon, when Didier came ashore. I was thinking of her. And of you," he added.

Dillon bit into a marshmallow. That explained some things. Perhaps his mother had been part loon. Dillon couldn't say it wasn't so. Or perhaps it was simply that her love came to him through them.

Before he went to bed, Dillon stood on the shore alone and uttered his last loon cry. It traveled across the lake, echoing off the distant hills, until it finally disappeared into nothingness.

21

FALLING ASLEEP WAS HARD. Staying asleep was worse. Dillon would wake and find himself straining to hear the loons' cry. Or he would think of the baby alone on the island. Of darkness and not knowing. It was not until after midnight that he closed his eyes.

At the first stirring of daybreak, Dillon rowed to the island. The baby loon was swimming circles in the cove. But it was not alone. Next to it was another loon, a bigger loon. Dillon watched as it dove under, brought up a fish, and fed it to the baby.

Dillon breathed a sigh of relief. He did not know where this new loon had come from and he did not care. But he knew that he would not have been able to catch a fish in his mouth and feed the baby. He would not have been able to convince this small bird that he was a loon. It was just as well that he wouldn't have to try.

Dillon pulled in his oars. The boat drifted closer to the cove. Dillon let out a low hoot and the baby loon looked at him. It did not cry back but moved closer to the bigger bird, who let out a shriek. At last it dove under, then bobbed to the surface seconds later. This made Dillon feel better. This was how it should be. He would not really have been a good parent to a loon. And in two weeks he would have to go back home. August had made its usual frank entrance. The leaves on the lake had begun to turn and a chill had settled in at night. School would be starting in a few weeks.

Dillon let the boat drift. Carried by the waves, it traveled closer to the island. Then the current changed. Dillon kept his eyes on the baby loon as long as he could. But before he knew it, he was drifting home.

Life went on. Didier was winding up the fishing season, cleaning and repairing his traps and equipment. Dillon rarely heard his magic flute anymore. Daisy had set Spencer free and was wanting a rabbit.

"A real one that I can play with," she said.

"And clean up after," added Dillon's mother. She turned to Dillon. "How about getting the mail?" she asked.

"Okay," said Dillon. It had been a long time since he had gotten the mail. He started up the dirt road. A grasshopper crossed his path. It had just one leg. It couldn't be the same grasshopper as before. But maybe it could, thought Dillon. How funny life was.

As Dillon neared the mailbox, he found himself hoping there might be something for him. He had not written anyone. He had not entered any contests. Still, he kept on hoping. He pulled down the door of the mailbox and reached for the small bundle inside. Two letters were for his father. There was a booklet of coupons and a newspaper. And there at the bottom of the pile was something for Dillon. An envelope with *Dillon Dillon* printed carefully in bright green ink. Dillon's heart bounded. He remembered when he'd gotten the letter from the cereal company with the free trip to Disneyland. But this was not an official letter. It was not on that kind of paper. Dillon opened it and read out loud.

Dear Dillon,

I thought I might see you again, but Lake Waban is a big place. Camp Tanglewood was terrific, though it was not really like a camp. There were bathrooms, televisions, and phones and a phone book. That's how I got your address. You are the only Dillons on Lake Waban. It is strange to write to someone who I met in line at a gas station bathroom. But I thought you looked very nice. Thank you again for the tiddlywink. If you give me your home address, maybe we can write and even see each other sometime.

Yours truly,

Eunice Schroeder
24 Woods Hole Drive
Northbridge, NH 03554

P.S. Why are you called Dillon Dillon?

Dillon had not expected this. But it was a great feeling. Eunice had given him her address. She did not live far from where he did. Eunice who had the same sneakers as he did. Eunice whose shirt rippled when she moved like the sun umbrella on the shore. Eunice with the bright smile. Eunice whose name had the word *nice* in it. And she had written to him. Dillon read the letter over and over again, feeling happier each time. Then he folded it carefully and put it back in the envelope. When he got home, he searched for a piece of paper and a pen and he wrote back.

Dear Eunice,

Thank you for your letter. It was a surprise. A good surprise. Did you know there are over five million tiddlywinks in the world? Do you still have the one I gave you? We have a sun umbrella the same color as the shirt you were wearing that day at the gas station. Lake W is a big place. There is an island near our cottage. I think you would like it. Maybe I could show it to you next summer. Your mother could meet me first and then I wouldn't be a stranger. Nor would you. Do you like Scrabble? Do you like birds? I hope

you do. You asked me why I am called Dillon Dillon.
It's a long story. But I'd be happy to tell you when we
meet.

Dillon sealed the envelope and put a stamp on it. He hoped Eunice would write back. Somehow he knew that she would.

"What are you writing?" Dillon's mother asked.

"A letter," said Dillon.

"To whom?" Dillon's mother asked.

"Just someone I met at a gas station," explained Dillon.

Dillon's mother smiled. But she looked worried. "A stranger?" she said. "If you write to strangers, you'd better be prepared for all kinds of weird responses."

"She's not a stranger," said Dillon. That was true. Or at least partially true. Eunice did not feel like a stranger. Her favorite color was green. She played tiddlywinks. Dillon felt like he'd known her all of his life.

22

DILLON DID NOT GO BACK to the island until just before he left. Instead he helped Didier paint his boat yet another time. He picked the last of the blueberries with Daisy. In the evenings he played chess with his father on the porch. He was becoming good at it.

"A penny for your thoughts," said his father one evening. He looked into Dillon's eyes and Dillon was reminded of the grasshopper, his mother, the loon. He knew, now, that the message in their eyes had been no different. They had simply been trying to tell him that love had no boundaries.

"You okay?" asked Dillon's dad.

"Yes," said Dillon. "I'm okay."

"It's been a long summer," said his dad.

Dillon nodded. "But a good one too," he added. Despite it all, that was how he felt. He felt it even more strongly when he pushed his boat into the water and rowed to the island for the last time.

The baby loon was still there in the cove. It had grown and was getting a full set of feathers.

Dillon stepped onto the island and moored the boat.

"Hey, fella," he called to the loon. The little loon looked up at Dillon. It had been afraid of Dillon at first. Now, when Dillon offered his hand, the loon swam up, stepped onto the shore, and waddled toward Dillon. Dillon waited to be pecked. But the loon did not peck him. Instead it slid back into the water, did a little foot waggle, and began aligning its feathers.

"You've grown," said Dillon, not realizing that anyone could have said the same thing about him.

Dillon reached into his pocket. He felt the sea-green tiddlywink. The one like he'd given to Eunice. The one Didier had found in the fish. He dug a hole in the sand and buried it. Perhaps it would find its way back to him or to Eunice or to someone else. Or maybe it would lie buried in the soil like his father's three silver coins.

"Goodbye, little fella," he said to the loon. "I've got to go back to school, back to Louis Gottlieb, back to being a boy."

The loon hooted loudly. It would be there until fall, until the frost came. Then it would leave for the winter. Dillon did not know where it would go. But he wondered if it would come back. He hoped it would. Dillon knew he would be back because that was his destiny.

The loon swam out into the lake. Dillon climbed back into his boat. He rowed away from the island slowly. It was hard to leave the loon. It would be even harder to leave the row-boat with *Dillon Dillon* painted in big ivory-colored letters on the stern. Dillon had traveled miles in that boat. He had taken a journey he would never forget. And his parents had let him go, knowing that he would come back. They had known him better than he knew himself.

Dillon headed home. Near the shore three miniature yellow sailboats flittered on the water.

Dillon's father had made them. One for each of the children, Daisy, Dillon, and Didier. Dillon studied them for a long time. When they were set free, they would bounce randomly on the surface of the water. Each had its own path, its own destiny. Sometimes they would bump up against one another. Other times they were carried far apart by the waves. And all this under the watchful eye of the sun.

Dillon hauled his boat onto the shore and joined his family. They feasted on the last corn of the season and blueberry pie. After supper they gathered on the front lawn. The evenings were shorter and colder.

"Put on your sweaters, everyone," said Dillon's mother. "You're going to catch cold." Not that she wasn't prepared. She had a first-aid box full of medicine and a cupboard lined with vitamins.

"Another summer gone," she added regretfully.

The last of the brown-eyed Susans had closed. Before they knew it, the frost would set in and life would grind to a halt for the winter months.

Dillon sat back in the canvas swing. The one that smelled like yellow and sunshine. Now it smelled like cool nights and blue shadows. He too felt a pang of regret at summer's end. His mind wandered over the events of the past few weeks. Eunice, the grasshopper, the island, the loons. His family. He looked at each of them now. Didier bent over a book on the picnic bench. Daisy chasing a squirrel. His mother sweeping up crumbs of blueberry pie with her hand. His father leaning back on his elbows in the grass. A wave of feeling swept over him and filled him with warmth. This would remain long after summer had left.

Daisy skipped over and buried her head in her father's lap. "Tell me a story," she said.

Dillon's father took a deep breath. His voice followed Dillon like a musical ribbon. "Once upon a time," he said.

"Once upon a time," repeated Dillon and he could not help but think of his own story and how it had begun. Once upon a time there was a boy named Dillon . . .